MAN FROM WYOMING

MAN FROM WYOMING

by

Dane Coolidge

The Golden West Large Print Books
Long Preston, North Yorkshire,
BD23 4ND, England.

British Library Cataloguing in Publication Data.

Coolidge, Dane
  Man From Wyoming.
  A catalogue record for this book is
  available from the British Library

ISBN   978-1-84262-949-9 pbk

Published in Large Print 2013 by arrangement with
Golden West Literary Agency

The Golden West Large Print is an imprint of Library Magna Books Ltd.

Printed and bound in Great Britain by
T.J. (International) Ltd., Cornwall, PL28 8RW

Chapter One

Night had laid a velvet hand over the bleak shacks of Powder Springs, endowing them with an illusion of beauty, and the half moon, up at midnight, cast long shadows across the street from the false fronts of stores and saloons. Swinging doors leaped open and closed, letting out winks of yellow light. The dance hall down the line was ablaze, but except for one man and the horses at the rack the straggling street was empty. The man came strolling down the walk from the dim hotel, humming a song to the clump of his boots, but as he passed the row of horses, he stopped in his stride and the song died on his lips. A ray of light, like the sudden stab of lightning, had swept the gaunt hip of a horse, and in that moment of illumination he had seen his own horse brand burned into the buckskin hide.

He glanced at the swinging doors of the Cowboy's Rest, whence the telltale light had come, and stepped out into the street. A match flared in his hand as he passed down the line, reading the brand on each roisterer's horse, and, as it bit his fingers, he threw it down with an oath and started back toward the saloon. But at the doorway he stopped short, pushing a swinging door ajar while he peered in at the noisy crowd.

'Rolling 'em high, eh?' he observed, closing the door on them grimly. 'No wonder the Lazy B has gone to hell.'

He racked off up the street in a stiff-legged gait that did not go with his city-made clothes, but as his boots woke the echoes of his old home town the song he had been singing came back.

While you are all so frisky
I will sing you a song.
I will take a horn of whisky
To help the song along.
It is all about a top screw
When he is busted flat
Sitting around town
In his Mexican hat.

There was more to the song that was not without its point, but as he neared the hotel, he saw a woman in its shadow – a woman cloaked in white, who turned and faced him defiantly.

'Why ... Penny!' he exclaimed after a moment of startled silence. 'What are *you* doing out here?'

'What are you doing?' she returned with a touch of annoyance. 'I was going out to see the town.'

He walked over closer and stood staring at her blankly. She was small and graceful, with exquisitely formed hands that fluttered and poised like butterflies, and in the pale light her face had an elfin look, as if she had come down on a moonbeam. Her eyes were big and blue with a suggestion of wondering innocence, but there had been something in her voice that was neither elfin nor innocent, and he towered above her accusingly.

'It's past midnight,' he said, 'and there's a bunch of cowboys in town. Does your mother know you're out?'

'She's asleep,' she defended, 'so what difference does it make? You won't tell her you saw me, will you?'

'Certainly not,' he promised, putting a protecting arm about her, 'but you mustn't go out alone.'

'Why not?' she pouted, pushing his hand away petulantly. 'Oh, Clay, can't I *ever* do *any*thing? It seems as if all my life, every time I start to do anything, somebody always drags me back and says ... don't!'

'Perhaps,' he replied, 'but you've struck a new country, where women are mighty scarce. Those cowboys are drunk, and they wouldn't understand it if they saw you on the street after midnight.'

'Well, *you* take me,' she pleaded, laying hold of his coat lapels and turning up her eyes appealingly. 'You used to live here,

Clay, and the cowboys would all know you.'

'It's a funny thing,' Clayton Hawks said. 'I just looked into that saloon, and there wasn't a man I knew. It's my own outfit, too ... they're riding Lazy B horses...'

'Do you love me?' she coaxed. 'Then take me down past there. I'm ... oh, I'm perfectly fascinated. And I know, with you with me, I'll be perfectly safe. Won't you do it, Clay, for me?'

'Well, all right, Penny' – he yielded as she gave him a kiss – 'but don't blame me if something awful comes off.'

'I won't,' she agreed, skipping along beside him. 'Didn't you ever feel the call of the wild? That's what's come over me ... or maybe it's the altitude ... but out here I just want to be free. I sat there in that stuffy room while Mother was going to sleep, and, oh, Clay, I couldn't stand it. I just had to get out and look up at the stars and feel that I was free.'

'It's the altitude,' observed Hawks, 'and this sagebrush smell. But don't overdo it at first.'

They passed down the silent street where the row of horses stood, and where the light shone out beneath the door, and then from the Cowboy's Rest there rose a savage yell like the howl of a pack of wolves.

'Let's be going,' muttered Hawks, but she held him against his will.

'It's the call of the wild,' she whispered.

'They're drunk!' he answered shortly.

'Come on, I'm going back.' And he drew her resolutely away. But as they passed the row of horses, she saw a broncho with head erect, rolling his eyes at the sound of the yells.

'Isn't it wonderful?' she sighed, stopping to watch him in the moonlight. 'Oh, Clay, I can't go back. What's that place down there,' she burst out eagerly, 'that house that's all lit up?'

'That's the hog-ranch,' he said. 'Not a very nice place. In fact, it's not respectable.'

'I'm tired of being respectable,' she burst out impatiently. 'If there's anything I hate, it's that word. Come on, I'm going down there.'

'You are not,' he declared. 'It's a bad house.'

'I don't care what it is,' she panted recklessly. 'I'm going down there, that's all.'

'Very well,' he said after a moment of tense silence. 'If you're going, I'll go along with you.'

She hesitated, then started down the road. He followed along behind her, waiting for her bad mood to pass, arguing angrily with her in his mind, but she stepped out boldly, now that the die was cast. There was a yell from uptown and the patter of horses' hoofs. Women's faces appeared at the doors, and then with a whoop a band of cowboys came rushing upon them, swinging their ropes and racing for the house. In the lead a

11

tall man was shaking out his loop, leaning forward as if marking down his prey, and with a cast incredibly swift he snapped the rope over Penny's head and jerked it up tight above her waist.

'That little white heifer is mine!' he yelled, and set his horse up with a flourish. The air was full of ropes, of hurtling forms and plunging mounts, as the tall man rode back through the dust, but as he was showing his big teeth in a triumphant laugh, Clayton Hawks laid hold of the rope.

'Just a moment,' he said. 'There's a slight mistake. This lady was just seeing the sights.'

'You drop that rope,' cursed the rider, 'or I'll bust your head open. I'll show her a good time myself.'

'Throw that loop off!' said Hawks, speaking over his shoulder to Penny as he set back to give her the slack, but she let the moment pass, and the rope bit into her flesh as the cowboy spurred back his mount.

'Drop that rope!' the cowboy warned, but Hawks had whipped out his jackknife and suddenly the taut reata snapped.

'There's ma honey!' grinned a huge Negro, flipping a deft loop at Penny's head the moment he saw the rope part.

But Hawks had seen his cast, and he plucked Penny away even before the tall cowboy could act. Then, as he rushed out and knocked the Negro from his horse, he shouted: 'You keep out of the affairs of a lady. What do you mean, butting in among decent folks?'

'I don't mean nuthin', suh,' answered the Negro apologetically. 'Jest havin' a little fun.'

'Dude, keep yourself out of this, understand?' ordered the cowboy arrogantly, wheeling his horse on Hawks. 'What do you mean,' he demanded, 'cutting my hogging strings like that? You limber-legged son-of-a-bitch, you ... git!'

He swung back the frayed end of his severed reata, but Hawks ducked its sweep and made a spring toward him. 'You get down off that horse, and I'll show you what I mean!' he answered as the crowd began to shout, and the tall man stepped down willingly.

They put up their fists, but as he faced his antagonist, the cowboy stepped back a pace. 'Say, who are you, anyway?' he asked uneasily. 'Your face seems kinda familiar.'

'I'm Clay Hawks! But don't let that make any difference. Step to it, if you think you can whip me.'

'Why ... Mister Hawks!' exclaimed the cowboy, suddenly sweeping off his hat and bowing to him and the lady. 'My Gawd, why didn't you tell me who you was? I wouldn't have had this happen for anything in the world ... and certainly beg your pardon, ma'am!'

He bowed once more to wide-eyed Penny, but Hawks stood looking at him dourly.

'What are you doing in town?' Hawks asked, ignoring the apology. 'You're supposed to be out riding the range. No wonder you lose eight hundred out of fourteen hundred steers... Dad sent me out here to see about it.'

'That is a matter of business, suh,' returned the Texan politely, 'that we can talk over better tomorrow, but I have made a great mistake in my treatment of this young lady, and I'd like to present my apologies.'

'That can wait until tomorrow, too,' replied Clayton Hawks curtly. 'Come, Penny, are you ready to go?'

'I'll give him back his rope first,' replied Penny, smiling bravely, and handed the bowing cowboy his loop.

Hawks glanced at her sharply, then reached out his hand and jerked the rope away. 'Haven't you got any sense?' he burst out angrily, and Penny seemed to shrink before him.

'Just a moment, suh,' pleaded the Texan gallantly. 'The fault was my own... I hope you'll not blame the young lady. And now, if you'll kindly introduce me, I'll present my apologies properly.'

Hawks looked him over coldly and shook his head. 'You'll never be introduced by me,' he stated.

'Beg pardon but I will,' returned the cowboy stubbornly. 'That's my right, as one gentleman to another.'

'You damned drunken sot!' exploded Hawks contemptuously. 'Where'd you get the idea you were a gentleman? I've got no business here myself, so I can't say too much, but is this the place you'd go to find a gentleman? This young lady is my fiancée, and she came out here under my protection, and I'll be damned if I'll introduce you!'

'Then I'll introduce myself,' spoke up Penny impulsively, and advanced with her hand outstretched. 'I'm Charlotte Pennyman,' she said, 'and it's all right about the rope. Can I keep this for myself?'

She held up the loop that Hawks had cast aside, and the cowboy bowed to the ground.

'My name is Jim Keck,' he said, 'and I ask a thousand pardons for my rough and discourteous treatment. Hawks is right ... I can hardly claim to be a gentleman.' He bowed again and, taking her dainty hand, raised it twice to his lips and was gone.

Chapter Two

'Give me that rope!' commanded Hawks as the lights faded behind them. 'And Penny, what in the world has come over you?'

'I don't know,' she faltered, but she held fast to the rope, and he knew that the madness still held her. If he pressed his demands, she would fight for her trophy, and yet what a shameful thing it was. In a normal mood she must recognize her error, but now she clung to the rope. It was the loop with which a man had taken her from the door of the hog-ranch, and yet, to her, it was the rope of a dashing Texas cowboy, the first real cowboy she had seen. They walked on in silence, and, as Hawks wrestled with this problem, his anger leaped from Penny to Keck.

Times had changed, indeed, when a man like that was superintendent of the Lazy B Ranch, yet that was the name of his father's new wagon boss, and Keck had remembered Hawks instantly. And now that he had seen him, Hawks remembered Keck as well, the first Texas cowboy to come to the Lazy B, and he had tried to live up to his name. But to demand an introduction to Penny! In a place where any gentleman would have hung his head for shame, to stand forth and brazenly ask that! Hawks's fist closed again, and he cursed the turn of fate that had made Keck remember him. And then, to make things worse, Penny had given the son-of-a-bitch her hand, and Keck had pressed it to his lips. This whole world seemed crazy and unreal.

'Please throw away that rope,' he ordered.

She glanced at him quickly and clutched it to her more tightly. 'It's my rope,' she said. 'He gave it to me.'

'It's my rope,' Hawks returned. 'Don't we own the Lazy B? Well, we supply all our cowboys with ropes.'

'You can't have it,' she replied, still watching him. 'All my life,' she went on slowly, as he made no move to seize it, 'I've been treated like a little child. From now on I'm going to be free.'

'It's a free country,' he observed grimly. 'A little too free. But I'll tame that bunch down ... tomorrow.'

'But Clay,' she protested, suddenly sensing his meaning, 'you aren't going to discharge him ... them?'

'That's my business,' he stated. 'There's something rotten about them or they wouldn't have lost eight hundred steers. I'll get to the bottom of it yet. And if you've decided to be free, I can see from tonight's experience that Wyoming is no place for *you*.'

'Why, *I* haven't been insulted,' she answered lightly. 'I wouldn't have missed it for anything. Can't you understand? Clay ... it's all so new to me, and Mister Keck wouldn't hurt me.'

'Don't you be so sure he won't hurt you.'

'Don't you worry,' she laughed. 'I'll look out for him.'

'Yes, and if that isn't being humiliated,' went on Hawks with rising wrath, 'I'd like to know what you call it. I'm dead sure *I* was humiliated, and if your mother ever hears about it...'

'Oh, but Clay, you promised not to tell.'

'She'll take you back to Boston,' he ended.

'I won't go!' she declared defiantly. 'I guess I'm of age. But, Clay, you won't tell her, will you?'

'I won't need to,' he reminded her, 'if she sees you with that rope. Won't you please throw it away and be sensible?'

'Oh ... well, *there* then!' she sobbed, slamming it down in the dust. 'You... I can't have my way about *anything.*'

Thinking it over later Clayton Hawks decided he had been hard-hearted, but when he got up in the morning and walked down to the store, the rope in the dust was gone. Two gaunt Lazy B horses, still at the rack of the Cowboy's Rest, swept away the last of his repentance. When he came to the office

18

of his father's resident managers there was a fighting light in his eye. William Bones might be honest and a good friend of the family, but he had sadly mismanaged the Lazy B. Not only had their calf tally shrunk twenty percent at a time when their neighbors' tallies were increasing, but of fourteen hundred steers, after two years on the range, they had shipped out only six hundred head. That had made even his father sit up.

The office of William Bones was a shabby old building, leaning up against one side of the bank, and the bank itself looked more like a powder house than the repository of Custer County's wealth. It was small and solidly built, with no pretentious plaster pillars to break the squat ugliness of its front, and there were those who said that the real business of the bank was transacted in Bones's back office. Certainly he was a director of the bank, and the sign on his window read *Loans and Investments* as well as *The 44 Cattle Company*.

Bones was sitting at a table behind his rolltop desk, pecking impatiently at a typewriter. As he looked up from his work, his projecting gray eyebrows were oddly suggestive of two bunches of sagebrush. His face was long and bony with a thick stand of bristling hair, and the stubble showed white on his chin.

'Well, mister?' he challenged in a voice

that made Hawks start, and then he rose up grimly. 'W'y, hello, Clay,' he said. 'Come out to investigate me? You're welcome, that's all I can say.'

He shook hands perfunctorily and dropped back in his chair again.

'Sit down,' he said. 'When'd you get in? Is your father still back there in Boston? Well, what's the difference if your mother did die ... he don't need to leave here for good. Don't you know, the greatest mistake Sam Hawks ever made was when he left that ranch. I've tried to look after it, and neglected my own business to keep things running smooth. But you just can't run another man's ranch and attend to your own affairs, too. My Snake-River outfit has been giving me no end of trouble ... they're wasting and stealing everything. Honestly, Clay, I don't know what I'd have done if it hadn't been for Jim Keck.'

'I see he's in town,' Hawks observed. 'What's going on ... been shipping some steers?'

'W'y, no,' replied Bones, rubbing his chin indecisively, 'but, well anyhow, he's a danged good man. Good cowman and a hard worker ... out riding day and night ... and he keeps the same men the year around. That's always a good sign with a boss. It shows his men are satisfied.'

'It's a good sign,' corrected Hawks, 'if his men are good men and if he keeps them out

20

on the job. But that's the hardest-looking bunch I ever encountered ... don't look like the old hands at all. And drunk and raising hell all over town. I brought two ladies out with me ... Missus Pennyman and her daughter ... and the first thing we saw, tied up at the Cowboy's Rest, was eight of my Lazy B horses.'

'You're not satisfied, then?' demanded Bones, screwing his mouth down and frowning. 'You don't like the way I've conducted things? Well, all right, Mister Hawks, if you think you can do any better, you're welcome to try your hand.'

'I'll begin,' nodded Hawks, 'by firing Keck.'

'You'll begin,' retorted Bones, 'by making one grand mistake. Things have changed since you left the ranch. You fire that man and the whole outfit will quit you right when you need men the worst. What will your father have to say to that?'

'Well,' began Hawks, and, as he stopped to consider, the move seemed a little ill-advised. Good cowboys were hard to get and the summer work was on – but his mind was made up about Keck. He would fire him the first chance he got. 'I'll look around,' he conceded, 'before I do anything radical. But what about those eight hundred steers?'

'Well, *what* about them?' demanded Bones, his harsh voice growing louder as he gloated over his initial victory. 'Do you think that you can find them? If you can, young man, I want to give you a gold medal, because I've had detectives on the job, and they failed. You may think that I've been negligent, and let things go to wrack and ruin, but you go out to that ranch and look around a while before you jump to any rash conclusions. I've got troubles of my own, and if it wasn't for your father, I'd never have undertaken the job. But I want to tell you right now that when William Bones accepts a trust, he lives up to the spirit of the agreement. This country has changed, I say, since you were out on the ranch. All the old men have got up and gone, and the hardest gang of cow thieves you ever saw in your life has moved in and settled in our midst. Right down in Coon Hole is the toughest bunch of citizens that was ever run out of the South, and the head and front of the gang is old Telford Payne, a rabid Secessionist even yet. He's a traitor to our government, and he's harboring a nest of outlaws just because they *are* against the government. There's the answer to your eight hundred lost steers.'

'Aha!' nodded Hawks. 'I didn't know about that. Has anything been done to get rid of him?'

'There's a lot you don't know,' observed Bones significantly. 'I knowed that the minute you opened your mouth. But since you're willing to listen, I'll tell you a few things more. Now you were asking about those eight hundred steers. This country has gone to hell till you'd hardly believe it, and train robbers and horse thieves are passing back and forth as common as Injuns used to be. They've got a regular Robbers' Trail from the Hole-in-the-Wall, up north, right down through Coon Hole and on south, and this rattlesnake Secesh is engaged in the business of buying and selling stolen stock. You can go down there yourself. I'm not asking you to take my word for it, but that man don't give a damn for the whole United States government, and he's crowded right in on my range.'

'On *your* range?' repeated Hawks. 'Why, I thought the Forty-Four was 'way over there on Snake River.'

'It is,' said Bones dryly, 'but I'm spreading out, understand? ... always did have a liking for Coon Hole. It's a fine winter range, sheltered and warm at all seasons, and there's Green River in times of drought. Lots of meadows to put up hay on, and except for the mosquitoes I don't know a thing against it ... the mosquitoes and Telford Payne. But I want you to go down there and look that outfit over ... they got those eight hundred steers, all right.'

'I'll go,' Hawks promised him, 'but if you're so positive they got them...?'

'Now there you go again!' burst out Bones.

'Why don't I get 'em back, eh? I'll tell you why I don't get 'em back. They're in Bear County, Colorado, and the sheriff over at Cody is a man that's got no business in office. He's afraid to go in there and arrest that gang of rustlers ... what can you do in a case like that? I've been trying all spring to slip a detective into Coon Hole and build up an ironclad case, but those ceder-snappers are too slick for me. They always run him out, and the last man they put a bullet through his pants. I'm glad you came back, Clay, because conditions are getting desperate, and they're pulling your cattle, right along.'

'They are, eh?' flared up Hawks, and Bones beamed triumphantly, but his smile vanished as Hawks went on. He had hoped for some oath of vengeance against the cedar-snappers of Coon Hole, but the Hawkses were always jumping some other way.

'Well, what's to prevent 'em,' Hawks burst out indignantly, 'with Keck and his whole outfit here in town? I don't like that man, Bones... I had a little run-in with him last night, and he's too damned polite to suit me ... and what I want to know is ... where does be get all this money that he's spending by the bootful across the bar? Did you pay him when they came in last night?'

'No ... I didn't,' acknowledged Bones, running his fingers through his hair while his eyes became fixed and grim. 'He's overdrawn his account already. Now it's strange ... I never thought of that before.'

'Well, I did, the first time I saw those horses at the rack. And here's another thing I thought of. It suddenly occurred to me in the watches of the night that they might be spending our steer money.'

'Ah, no,' dissented Bones, shaking his shaggy head vigorously, 'you're too suspicious. You're prejudiced against Keck. But now you mention the subject, I don't mind telling you in strictest confidence that I had, the same idee myself once. Never tempt a man too far ... that has always been my favorite motto. So last fall, after that shortage in the steer shipment came up, I sent an old trapper out to Keck. No harm, you understand, to find out what's going on, and this old wolfer could kinder keep an eye out. But no, by Gawd, Keck wouldn't have him around ... said he'd kill more beef than the varmints. And now ain't that the truth? I decided right there that Keck savvied his business.'

'He savvied trappers, all right,' conceded Hawks, still unconvinced, 'but maybe he was protecting himself.'

'Oh, if you go as far as that,' growled Bones impatiently, 'they ain't any of these cowboys you can trust. They'd all steal and lie, and sit up all night playing poker, and come to town and go on a drunk, but out on the ranch, I tell ye, this Keck is an A-One boss. He runs that wagon to perfection. Every one of his men is an experienced 'puncher that can write his name with a running iron, and I'll bet you'll find your calves branded up clean and slick ... so what more can you ask and expect?'

'You may be right,' responded Hawks after a long and thoughtful silence, 'but at the same time I'm against keeping Keck. I don't like him, and never will, so why not give him his time and get some man we can trust? Say! What's become of Rooster Raslem? There's a man that I'd trust anywhere ... a good hand, and absolutely honest. And never drank a drop... I used to run with him myself, when we came to town with the boys, and I know he was sober as a judge.'

'All the same,' returned Bones with a broken-toothed smile, 'you'd better leave well enough alone.'

'Ah, but Rooster was a prince,' went on Hawks enthusiastically, 'and a natural cow-man, too. He taught me all I know about handling cattle, and he was always getting off some joke. Say, what became of him, any-way?'

'We-ell,' evaded Bones, 'he worked for the Lazy B a while, and then he had a run-in with Keck. He came over and rode with me for a while ... I had to give him his time. So you think he was absolutely honest?'

'I know it,' pronounced Hawks. 'There's a man I'd trust anywhere.'

'Well, that shows how much you know about picking a wagon boss. Rooster Raslem is now a fugitive from justice.'

'I don't believe it!' exclaimed Hawks. 'There must be some mistake. You can't tell me Rooster's gone wrong.'

'Oh, I can't, hey?' returned Bones, beginning to fumble in his disordered desk. 'Well, just cast your eye on that!'

He flipped over a crumpled circular with Raslem's photograph smiling out from it and looked up at Clayton Hawks through his eyebrows. 'Five thousand dollars reward,' he quoted oracularly, 'for Horace Plunkett, alias Rooster Raslem, wanted for train robbery. On the night of April Third, in company with Sundance Thorp... '

'I don't believe it,' Hawks answered sullenly.

'All right,' returned Bones, 'you don't have to believe it ... but what about making him our wagon boss?'

'That's impossible now, of course,' returned Hawks sharply. 'Is there anybody you'd like to suggest?'

'I suggest Keck ... and I suggest further, Mister Hawks, that you keep your hands off this business. Those boys are working for me, and they come to me for orders... '

'Well, order them out of town, then,'

snarled Hawks.

He rose up, his eyes glowing, and after a mocking smile William Bones also rose, reaching over for his hat. They passed out into the bright sunlight, Bones hustling along in the lead while Hawks followed behind, and the search for Keck began. At the Cowboy's Rest, the barkeeper hadn't seen him and a drunken 'puncher said he was over at the hog-ranch. At the hog-ranch the madame informed them that Keck had been there but had gone back to town.

'Down at the corral,' suggested Bones at a black look from Hawks, and strode off faster than ever. He was a big, long-legged man, clad in rusty brown clothes and with a meager, boy's-size hat on his head, and, instead of the trim boots that his cow-punchers wore, he was shod in broad-toed shoes. As he hurried through the sand, Clayton Hawks was gradually left behind, and, when he reached Main Street, Hawks met Bones coming back, but without any sign of Keck.

'Now, see here,' Hawks accosted him, 'let's end this farce. That rounder is not fit...'

'He's the best man in these parts,' defended Bones irascibly, 'if you can keep the danged fool out of town. But I know where he's at. There's a married woman down below here...'

Bones ground his teeth with rage and

paced off faster than ever, but, as he passed the hotel, he stopped short. Hawks came up behind him, and they both gazed through the hotel window – for there sat Keck, talking to Penny. Mrs Pennyman sat beside them, smiling blandly at what he was saying, and across Penny's lap lay the rope loop.

Chapter Three

A man meets trouble in one way and a woman in another. Charlotte Pennyman looked out, and beckoned radiantly. Keck flinched and glanced behind him. Mrs Pennyman still sat beaming. Out in the street Hawks and Bones stood staring.

'Who's that woman?' demanded Bones with instant suspicion. 'God damn that cuss Keck. I could kill him!'

'He'll get killed,' predicted Clayton Hawks, 'if he carries this much further. Mister Bones, that young lady is my fiancée.'

'Your which?' scowled Bones.

Before Hawks could explain, Penny leaped up and flung open the door. 'Come on in, Clay!' she called 'We've been looking for you everywhere. We're going right out to the ranch. Oh, it's all arranged.' She laughed as he gazed at her blankly. 'Is this Mister

Bones, the manager?'

She shot out a hand, and Bones crushed it in sheer amazement.

'What did you say the name was?' he cried harshly.

'Charlotte Pennyman,' she smiled, twisting one hand in her dress and glancing up at him shyly. 'Mister Keck has been telling us all about you.'

'Oh, he has, has he?' spoke up Bones, suddenly coming out of his trance and assuming a rough good-nature. 'Well, if I'd tell you what I know about Mister Keck...'

'You'd be ashamed to be caught dead with him,' finished Hawks. He meant it, every word. Penny knew that he meant it, but she had the game in hand and could afford to ignore his spite.

'Come in,' she invited Bones, 'and say it to his face. Mister Keck has been saying *nice* things about you. Meet my mother, Mister Bones ... you know Mister Keck.'

'What was the name?' broke in Bones, stopping awkwardly in front of Mrs Pennyman, and that lady placed him at a glance.

'Missus Pennyman,' she repeated with gracious distinctness, and turned to the courtly Keck. 'Won't you go on, please,' she beamed. 'What you were saying was very interesting. Please sit down, Penny ... and *stop* picking on Clay.'

Penny bowed her head obediently, then

30

sank back into a chair, and turned adoring eyes upon Keck. The marks of last night's excesses showed all too plainly on his heavy face, and his eyes were puffed and blood-shot, but the hand in which he held a slender, beaded glove was as white and well-groomed as a lady's. His dark hair was oiled and brushed, his mustache tightly waxed, his clothes of the best cloth and cut, and his boots and spurs were all that money could buy – he was exquisite, right off the range.

Clayton Hawks gazed at him contemptu-ously, yet noting the powerful arms and the set of his shoulders and neck. In a rough and tumble fight he would be a hard man to deal with, in spite of his dandified airs. But it was his voice and his masterful smile, his perfect self-possession, that held the women to the end of the tale. Hawks and Bones both scorned even to listen to him.

'Now, here,' broke in Bones, the moment the story was ended, 'I came up on a matter of business. Mister Keck, you round up your men and get out of town ... there's work for you to do on the range.'

'Very well,' bowed Keck, rising to his feet on the instant. 'I hope the ladies will excuse me.'

'Oh, but he was going to drive us to the ranch,' protested Penny, flying at Bones reproachfully. 'I don't think it's fair...'

'Another time, Miss Penny,' consoled

Keck from the doorway. 'I've got to round up my cowboys now.'

He stepped out swiftly, striding off down the street to the clank of his silver-mounted spurs.

'Well, guess I'll go,' Bones announced to Hawks. 'Anything more that I can do?'

'Just a moment,' called Hawks as Bones slammed out the door, but Penny rushed in before him.

'Mister Bones,' she said, 'you have charge of the ranch, haven't you? Mister Keck said that you did. Well, wouldn't it be all right if Mother and I went out there? He said we could live in the rooms back of the cook house, if old Uncle Simmy would move out.'

Bones glanced at Hawks, and then at Mrs Pennyman who was beaming upon him amiably.

'Why, yes, yes,' he stammered, 'you're friends of Clay's, ain't ye? Then, of course, it's all right, with *me*!' He glanced at Hawks again, for he still stood there, grim and silent, and ventured an inept joke. 'What's the matter, Clay?' he smirked. ''Fraid Keck will cut you out? Well, if he does, you know what you can do ... you can fire him.'

'I can fire him right now,' returned Hawks, and something told them he intended to do it.

'Why, Clayton!' exclaimed Mrs Pennyman in shocked surprise, 'we thought he was perfectly lovely.'

'He is,' broke in Bones with a loud guffaw.

Hawks whirled upon him angrily. 'Mister Bones,' he said, 'you're not called in on this, at all. I'll talk the matter over with Missus Pennyman.'

'Heh! Techy this morning,' commented Bones sarcastically and Penny met his eye and smiled. He winked at her knowingly as he scuttled out the door, and Penny turned back with a sigh.

'Oh, Clay,' she scolded, 'what's the matter with you? Don't you want anybody to have a good time?'

'I'll just take that rope,' he said, and she stepped back, one hand behind her. Her eyes, which had been so round and innocently appealing, suddenly took on a wild, startled look, and then they changed again. It brought back to Hawks's mind the vision of a horse that once had slipped its halter on the plains – the horse had not moved, but a new look had come into its eyes when it knew that it was free. And now Penny did not move, only her eyes lighted up, and she gazed at him demurely. Hawks wondered why he had ever loved her.

'Why, Clayton,' soothed Mrs Pennyman, 'what is the matter this morning? Have you been having a quarrel with Penny?'

'Not yet,' he said, 'but I want that rope. Did she tell you how she got it?'

'Why, yes!' she exclaimed. 'It was rather unusual, but I see nothing for you to be angry about. Don't you like her acquaintance with Mister Keck?'

'No, I do not,' he answered.

Penny drew back a step. Then with the swiftness of a whirlwind she flung up the stairs and slammed the door of her room.

Mrs Pennyman looked at Hawks and motioned him to a chair.

'What is the matter? I don't understand.'

Hawks sat down absently and remained gazing into space.

'Neither do I,' he said at length. 'What did she tell you about the rope?'

'Why, this rope, as I understand, was given to her last night after she had met Mister Keck at the dance hall. It seems that he and his cowboys came charging down upon the place just as the girls came out of the hall, and Mister Keck, seeing Penny, naturally thought that she was one of them and lassoed her to be his partner. But when it was explained that she was just an Eastern visitor, of course he was greatly chagrined so, taking out his knife, he cut his rope in two, as a penance, you might say, for his rudeness. I thought it was really quite romantic.'

'Yes,' Hawks grunted and sat silent. 'Was that all?' he asked at last.

'Why, no,' she went on, 'she told about meeting you, and of your objection to her being out at night. But really, Clayton, you mustn't judge her too harshly.'

'Missus Pennyman,' he burst out hoarsely, 'don't let me or anybody fool you ... this country is no place for a woman. I had no business to ever bring you out here. But my advice to you now is to take Penny and go back ... and, for God's sake, don't go out to the ranch.'

'No!' cried Penny, flying down the stairway from where she had been listening over the banister. 'Now Mother, don't you believe a word he says. He's just doing this out of spite, because Mister Keck was nice to us, but I'm going out ... to ... that ... ranch!'

She beat her hands on the table in childish passion, and her mother smiled at her mildly.

'Penny, dear,' she said, 'you should not be so insistent. It's Clayton's ranch and he hasn't even asked us.'

'Well, if he's as mean as all that...!' She clutched the engagement ring that Hawks had so recently given her, drew it off, and then thrust it back. 'I don't care,' she sobbed. 'I'm going.'

'You can go,' spoke up Hawks after a minute of heavy silence, 'if...'

'No ifs!' she exulted, reaching his side at a bound and kissing his uncompromising lips. 'You're a Yankee through and through, Clayton Hawks. But we're out West now, where the winds of freedom blow ... don't you think you can trust your lucky Penny?'

She ruffled up his hair until she made him laugh, and the *if* was lost in the scuffle. But when he stepped out and saw Keck up the street, Clayton Hawks suddenly wondered if he could trust his lucky Penny? And would she bring *him* luck?

As he stood in meditation, heavy footsteps came hurrying toward him, and Bones's voice rasped in his ear.

'Say,' he demanded, 'who air them womenfolks anyway?'

'They belong,' replied Hawks, 'to one of the best families of Boston. Missus Pennyman is an old friend of my father's.'

'Yes, but the girl,' persisted Bones, 'what was that French word you called her?'

'Oh, my fiancée ... that means we're engaged.'

'You don't say!' exclaimed Bones, slapping his leg hilariously. 'Well, why didn't you tell me in the first place? Is that what your father took you back to Boston fur? Or was it to learn this here French? How'd you come out ... is she going to the ranch?'

'Yes, she's going,' Hawks nodded as Bones burst into a guffaw, 'but please try to restrain yourself, Mister Bones. Because if you don't' – he flared up – 'I'm liable to bust you over the head and take charge of the outfit myself.'

'Oh, you air, hey?' responded Bones, suddenly straightening his face out. 'Well, what can I do for you, *Mister* Hawks?'

'You can call up that man Keck,' Hawks answered evenly, 'and give him his orders in my presence. Otherwise, I'll do it myself. You tell him to take his wagon and go ahead with his range branding, and, if I catch him around that ranch house, I'll fire him so damned quick...'

'Hey! Jim!' shouted Bones. 'Come over here!'

Keck cantered over briskly, riding a beautiful, glossy bay that fought its head yet yielded to his mastery.

'Jim,' began Bones, 'I want you to understand right now that Mister Hawks is going to be your boss. His father has sent him out here to look into the loss of those steers, so the ranch will still remain in my charge. But whatever he says ... goes ... as far as you are concerned ... or me, too, for the matter of that.'

'Very well, seh,' returned Keck. 'I shall endeavor to please you both, but any time, Mister Bones, that my services ain't satisfactory...'

'Aw, no, no,' broke in Bones impatiently, 'you're all right, as long as you stay out of town ... but this carousing around will have to stop, and I want you to keep in your place. You're not employed, Jim, as a professional entertainer or to make up to Mister Hawks's private guests. You're hired ... and don't you forget it ... to run that wagon and brand-up them Lazy B calves. Mister Hawks naturally asked, when he had seen your men in town, what was to prevent them Coon Hole rustlers from stealing him blind ... and I had to tell him, Jim ... not a god-damned thing! You ain't been treating me right.'

Keck shifted in his saddle and looked up the street, where one of his 'punchers had just fallen off his horse.

'Maybe not, suh,' he admitted, but without remorse. 'Anything more, before I go?'

'Now about them steers,' charged Bones, raising his voice to a fighting pitch, 'they've jest got to be found, that's all. I want you to do everything in your power to help Mister Hawks find that stuff. Eight hundred big steers, worth twenty dollars a head at least, out of fourteen hundred head shipped in. We jest can't stand it, that's all. It don't pay. It's ruinous. We'll be bankrupt, and it shows some negligence, somewhere.'

'Well now, Mister Bones,' began Keck argumentatively, 'I beg leave to differ with you there. It shows no negligence on my part. I've rode down a mount of horses trying to locate them steers, and I can't find hide nor hair of 'em.'

'No negligence?' stormed Bones. 'You're here in town, ain't you? What business have *you* got in Powder Springs? And what's to

38

prevent Tel Payne and that bunch of Coon Hole cow thieves from stealing every critter we've got?'

'I've got two men, seh,' defended Keck, 'in my line camps down on the Alkali, throwing the stuff back toward the ranch. But when it comes to Coon Hole, that's one place I decline to go into ... not for no hundred dollars a month.'

His eyes flashed with sudden fire, and then became set as Bones thrust out his jaw and began to rant.

'Not for no hundred dollars,' repeated Keck with finality. 'When a sheriff and two deputies say that outfit is too hard for 'em, and decide they cain't find any rustlers...'

'That sheriff is a coward!' Bones shouted furiously. 'He ought to be kicked out of office! And he will be ... the next election. And when he is, mind ye, I'll have the law on them cedar-snappers. I'll put old Tel Payne in prison. I'll put a ring in his nose, the Secesh son-of-a-bitch, if it costs me every dollar I've got ... he's stealing my Forty-Four cows, too!'

'Jest a moment, seh,' said Keck, 'them boys are trying to kill one of my men.' He spurred over to the Cowboy's Rest, where a fight was in progress, and Bones rolled his eyes at Clayton Hawks. 'Now, you see?' he nodded. 'That's jest what we're up against. Them steers have disappeared into Coon Hole.'

39

'I'll get 'em,' promised Hawks, 'if they're there.'

'You'll get killed,' predicted Bones, smiling approvingly.

Chapter Four

'It's going to be grand,' spoke up Penny ecstatically as Hawks was driving her and her mother out to the ranch. 'I feel so free already.'

In the distance there rose dim ranges whose names Penny did not know but which reminded her of mountains seen in dreams. They held clouds upon their shoulders, and their ramparts were huge and square like fortresses hewn from solid rock. Behind the eastern horizon snowcapped peaks thrust up their heads, long mesas stretched away into the heat, and across the soft gray flats the shadows of drifting clouds floated in silently from the west.

Hawks roused up at Penny's words as if he had been struck – where was it leading to, all this talk about being free? Did she plan, at the ranch, to get a horse and run wild as so many Eastern tourists did, making friends with all the cowboys, committing unheard of indiscretions, while he stood by and looked on like a fool? There was work for him to do, perhaps a fight on his hands, and the woman would be an incubus at best. If Penny's visit was to be the occasion of further harebrained escapades, he saw his whole mission brought to naught. He would have to stay at home and ride herd on her like a duenna, getting little if any thanks for his pains, and meanwhile the Lazy B steers were being run off by the hundreds, with nobody but him to stop it.

'Yes,' he replied, 'it's a free country, all right, but even that has certain disadvantages. Lots of men out here would be making hair bridles in the penitentiary if the officers were half on their jobs.'

'I am surprised,' observed Mrs Pennyman, following her own line of thought, 'that your father should ever have settled here. Such a wild, desolate country, without a single tree in sight ... how far is it, Clayton, to the ranch?'

'Twenty miles, by the road. We go clear out to that point and then back when we get up on top ... the boys ride right straight across.'

He pointed due south where a line of tiny dots marked the galloping flight of his cowhands, and once more Penny sighed.

'Will they be there when we arrive?' she asked at last.

He shrugged his shoulders gloomily. 'Very

likely,' he said. 'Drunk, tough, and disorderly, whooping and hollering and raising Hades all night. Either that or they'll hook up and go out on the mesa to sleep it off away from the house. All depends on which way they jump.'

'Will it be perfectly safe?' asked Mrs Pennyman doubtfully. She appeared in the sunlight a large, placid woman with yellowed white hair and an expression of Buddha-like calm.

Penny burst out laughing, almost recklessly. 'I hope they stay,' she said. 'I want to see them ride some bronchos. Did you notice that big Negro, Mother? Well, Mister Keck tells me that he's the best broncho rider in the West and Mister Bones told me that Mister Keck is a horse *tamer* ... he can make any of them perfectly gentle.'

'Isn't that wonderful,' beamed Mrs Pennyman 'Are you a good rider, too, Clayton? I should think you'd be afraid of them. But I noticed that Mister Keck has a very gentle way about him, and I suppose that even horses understand.'

'Yes, they understand,' said Hawks, and let the subject drop for it brought up ugly thoughts. Perhaps he had been stubborn and in a way, unreasonable in his objections to Penny's conduct with Keck, but he felt even yet an angry resentment at the way she had flouted his judgment. She had taken advantage of his absence to meet Keck a

42

second time and get herself invited to the ranch, and then she had arrayed Bones and her mother against him until he had had no choice but to yield. And now that she had her wish and was on her way to the ranch, she was suddenly quiescent again.

He glanced over at her curiously, as if looking at a stranger, and wondered if he really knew her. Men had lived, so he had heard, the full span of their lives with women whose minds they never fathomed, until, in some crisis, the truth had come out, and they discovered some greater love – or hate. It was something Bones had said that had summoned up these uneasy thoughts – had his father taken him East for a purpose? Did he have in his mind this alliance with Charlotte Pennyman when he had insisted upon taking his son to Boston? Hawks had not missed that movement when Penny had snatched off her ring, and he had been surprised that he had steeled his heart to accept it if, to gratify some whim, she threw the token of their engagement at his feet. He looked at her, her childish face rapt and smiling as she gazed across the plain, and the grim lines relaxed as he watched. She was an Easterner – and he was a Westerner.

The Hawkses were a stern breed and, where women were concerned, perhaps a little exacting and hard – his father had been that way – but, given their own way, they had not proved impossible. It was only when they were crossed that they grew stubborn. Clayton Hawks cursed his hard heart as he glanced again at the yellow hair, the drooping eyelashes, the blue, brooding eyes. Such women were to be petted and wooed away from their caprices, for at heart she was still a child.

Out across the rolling prairie they proceeded at a brisk trot, their trunks lashed securely behind, and, as the long line of Hawks Mesa rose up before them, the road swung off to the west. Under the brow of a high point where a break in the sandstone capping made way for a gradual ascent, the grade wound laboriously up until at last, winning the summit, they looked out over the broad tableland beyond. Surrounded on every side by its high wall of sandstone, it was a stronghold easily kept, and Sam Hawks had been a man to hold his own in any country, whether his enemies were many or few. No sheep had ever grazed on this ocean of waving grass, no predatory cattlemen had invaded his domain, and over the edge of the cup – for the mesa was bowl-shaped – his winter range extended on to the south. It was an empire, almost taken and held by one man, and like all empires subject to decay. Once his strong grip was slackened, disintegration would set in – already they were stealing his steers – but the time had not arrived when the kingdom could be divided for the heir apparent still lived. Clayton Hawks sat silently as his eyes swept the familiar plain, seeking out each water hole and branding ground, and then he turned to his guests.

'This is the ranch,' he said, 'as far as you can see. Headquarters is down there where you'll notice those white spots ... we'll be there now in two hours.'

'How far everything is!' exclaimed Mrs Pennyman in dismay. 'Really, Clayton, it almost frightens me. And to think that your father would shut himself up here and waste the best years of his life.'

'Shut himself up?' repeated Hawks. 'Seems to me this is outdoors. I felt shut up back in Boston.'

'I mean isolate himself,' defended Mrs Pennyman stoutly. 'All this land, and only one house.'

'And a bum house at that,' observed Hawks. 'You'll wish yourself back at the hotel.'

'Not that hotel...' began Mrs Pennyman, but Penny spoke up louder.

'I won't,' she said. 'I want to live here always.' But she did not meet Hawks's answering smile. Did she mean, then, live there with him?

They drove on down the long slope to where the upheaval of the rim had cracked the solid formation of the sandstone, forming a series of water holes and springs. Round-bellied cattle stood by the water, lazily fighting the flies. A band of rangy horses ran off. After toiling on and on through sand and bog and sagebrush, they came within sight of the ranch. It was a group of log buildings placed about a huge spring hole whose waters, running off, formed a pond, and in the dirt of the mud roofs grew grass and gnarly cactus as if to typify the meagerness of their life. Huge corrals and feeding racks and stables roofed high with hay intervened between the houses and the gate, and it seemed as if in that place cattle and horses were everything and human beings little or nothing. A humped-back old man stepped out of the cook house and, wiping his hands on his apron, regarded them apathetically.

'They're gone!' mourned Penny, looking around for the cowboys, and then she leaped to the ground. 'But we're here,' she nodded cheerily. 'Good afternoon, Uncle Simmy. Do you think you can take us in?'

Uncle Simmy looked at her a trifle longer than was necessary and spat out a quid of tobacco. 'Boss' orders,' he answered in a thin, discontented whine. 'He left a horse for you, out in the corral.'

'Oh, did he?' she exclaimed. 'I'm going out to see it!' And she dashed back to the high, pole corral.

'I'm Mister Hawks,' said Hawks formally.

'Let me introduce you to Missus Penny-man. Jim Keck didn't mention your name.'

'No matter,' mumbled the cook, 'let it go for Uncle Simmy. Glad to meet you, ma'am.' He bowed to Mrs Pennyman.

She responded a trifle stiffly, for her eyes had strayed past him into the house that was to be their Western home. The entrance was through the kitchen, there being no door at the north end on account of the winter blizzards, and from what she could see of Uncle Simmy and his abode she did not imagine she would like it.

'Jest step in, ma'am,' he invited, a trace of hostility in his voice, 'and I'll show you to your room. We ain't no ways fixed, of course, to entertain womenfolks...'

'Oh, it's all right, I'm sure,' she said hopefully.

'But it's the best we've got,' he ended.

They passed through the dining room, with its oilclothed table and long benches, into what had all too evidently been Uncle Simmy's den. As Hawks looked around at the crude and dirty bedroom, he glanced at Mrs Pennyman expectantly. She would know now what he had meant when he had advised her in Powder Springs to wait until quarters could be prepared for her, but after a quick glance about she said it would do nicely, at which Uncle Simmy disappeared. He had been compelled by their advent to move out to the bunkhouse, where his tobacco would be at the mercy of thieving cowboys, but his expression, as he fumbled about throwing together a belated supper, indicated a gloomy resignation to his fate.

Hawks moved to the bunkhouse, too, for this room that the Pennymans now shared had once been his and his father's. The cook had moved in since they left.

It required only a glance to indicate to Clayton Hawks the depredations his absence had brought. The door to this bedroom had been solidly padlocked, since it housed their papers, but now the lock was gone and prying hands had soiled and desecrated the keepsakes and books along the wall. The bed was broken down, the floor hacked and filthy with old magazines thrown carelessly about, and there was apparently not a single sheet to cover up the greasy bedding. It was shocking, but Hawks had warned them, and he left them to fight it out. Complaisant mothers must expect such dilemmas when they indulged their daughters too far.

Breakfast was served at daylight at the Lazy B Ranch, and Uncle Simmy saw no reason to make a change. He routed them out promptly at a quarter after four, and breakfast consisted of coffee, bacon, and flapjacks. Hawks had discovered in the cook the evening before that same aloofness he had noted in Keck, and he saw in this contrariness an overweening determination to smoke the ladies out of his room. The fact that he, Clayton Hawks, was the son of the owner did not deter the cook any more than it did Keck, and he detected in both a surly antagonism – an eagerness, almost, to get fired. But the time had not yet come to make a change of cooks, and Hawks accepted things as a matter of course. Penny came to her breakfast in riding boots and spurs, talking of nothing but the horse Keck had left, and immediately after the meal she unpacked her Western saddle and gave Hawks no peace until she was mounted. Then she galloped off down the road, just as he had expected from the first, leaving her mother gazing helplessly after her.

'Well there!' she exclaimed to Hawks. 'I hope the child is happy. She's been looking forward to this moment for months.'

An ecstasy that was almost madness seemed to lay hold upon Penny as she spurred her flying pony across the plain, but after the first burst she reined him in to a walk, and at last she rode back to the ranch.

'Where are the cowboys?' she asked as she found Hawks rigging his own saddle. 'Come on, let's go out where they are!'

The impulse to refuse, to oppose her in everything, rose up as he met her eager eyes, but something about their appeal suddenly smote his heart with pity, and he fought down his jealousy of Keck. They had come to a new world, and Penny was entitled to her fling, provided it did not take her too far. Besides, something told him that this Penny was a different woman from the sheltered and petted child he had known. The wild look had come back, the daring, resolute gleam that he had noted the day before, and he knew, if he opposed her, she would start off by herself, like the horse that had slipped its halter on the plains. She was free, and it had gone to her head.

'All right,' he said, and half an hour afterwards they were following the deep tracks of the wagon wheels.

'Let's gallop!' she cried, giving her horse his head, and once more he gave in to her. She rode well on the swift sorrel that Keck had left for her, so well that she left Hawks behind, and, when he spurred over a roll, he saw her below him, trotting up to the Lazy B wagon. It was parked in a swale, and, although the morning was half gone, the cowboys were just roping out their mounts. Tied to two wheels of the wagon the long cavvy ropes stretched out, making a corral to hold the rope-shy horse herd. While two men guarded the stakes that held up the outside corners, the tall Texans flipped their loops into the rout. At every lash of the rope there was a rush and a thunder of hoofs, then a hush as the noose found its mark. As Hawks rode up unnoticed, he saw Keck coming out, leading a horse that fought its head and stepped high. Penny was looking on admiringly, her eyes big with delight, and all the rough Texans were grinning.

'Will he *buck?*' repeated Keck after she had shot out the eager question. 'Why, yes, I reckon he will.'

'Well, make him!' she urged. 'I just want to see him ... that is, if he won't buck too hard.'

'Hard or easy,' laughed Keck, 'it's all the same to me. I allow I can ride 'most any of 'em.'

'Please ride him, then,' she said, and he glanced up at her teasingly.

'I'll ride one if you will,' he challenged.

'All right!' she answered gaily, and Keck nodded at Hawks, who had ridden up beside his affianced. 'Shall I ride one for the lady?' he inquired, and at the word he threw on his saddle and mounted.

The horse stood rigid, his head held high, waiting the touch of the reins to be gone, and Keck smiled as he took off his hat.

'This is going to surprise him some,' he observed to Penny and slapped the horse full in the face. At the smash of the hat the horse whirled and shook his head, and the Texans let out a yell.

'Hook 'im!' they shouted, and Keck threw

forward a gleaming spur and raked him from neck to flank. Down went the horse's head, and in a series of writhing jumps he bucked across the flat and stopped. Keck sat him like a statue, swaying his body to meet each lunge, balanced as nicely as a mannequin on a pivot.

'Oh, ride him some more!' called Penny in a frenzy, but he shook his head and came back.

'We're a little late,' he apologized. 'Have to be starting now, I reckon. Come out again sometime and we'll ride a real bronc'.'

'Then it's my turn,' she said, dropping down from her horse. 'I'll bet I can ride him, all right.'

'I don't doubt it, ma'am,' he smiled as the cowboys all shouted, 'but you might get hurt, you know.'

'No. I mean it,' she declared, struggling to strip off her saddle, and Keck glanced inquiringly at Hawks.

'Let her ride him,' Hawks said quietly, and Penny whirled about and faced him.

'I didn't ask your permission,' she said.

'I was speaking to Mister Keck,' he answered, still quietly. 'I know there's no use talking to you, Penny.'

She gave him another look and turned to the waiting Keck.

'You'd better not ride him,' he suggested. 'He's a worse horse than he looks, ma'am, and, when he gets excited, he's got a dirty way of falling over backwards. Some other time, Miss Penny, when you've had a little more practice ... not that I doubt you can ride him. You certainly have got the nerve.'

'Well,' began Penny, looking the broncho over doubtfully, 'perhaps you're right, Mister Keck ... I won't.'

She stood glaring after them as they rode off on the circle, and then she turned on Hawks. 'Don't you think I dared to ride him?' she demanded furiously.

'I don't know, Penny,' he answered. 'You certainly are acting very strangely. All I knew was you wouldn't listen to *me*.'

'I don't have to listen to you,' she flared back resentfully. 'Mister Keck must think that you own me.'

'Very well,' he said. 'You're free.'

'It's a free country,' she quoted, and was laughing recklessly when she caught the glint in his eye.

'I wonder,' he said, 'if you realize that *I* have not been free?'

It was the way he said it, more than what he said, that made Penny go suddenly pale. 'What is it?' she demanded. 'What do you mean?'

'I mean,' he said, 'I'm going to take you back to town. There's such a thing as being too free.'

Chapter Five

The castles in the air, the long days of life and freedom she had counted as good as won, fell away before his words like a mirage. Where before she had glimpsed freedom and wild gallops across the plains, she saw the gray streets of Boston with the people plodding decorously to church. The dream broke and left her staring, then the bitter tears came, and she leaned against her horse and sobbed.

'I won't go!' she cried rebelliously, but, when she met his steady eye, she knew she had tried him too far. He knew all her pretty tricks, her sudden tears and childish endearments, and his mind was firmly set on one thing – he would take her away from Jim Keck. Merely to win the form of freedom she had cast away its reality – she was to be sent home like a schoolgirl. She swung up on her pony and galloped back toward the ranch, but the glory had gone out of the morning that at dawn had seemed the fairest in her life. This man whom she had twisted like a ring about her finger had ruined it all with a word. A hundred desperate expedients rose up in her mind to escape from this pit she had dug, and then with a stifled sob she reined in her horse and waited to make her peace. She knew now that she was not free.

Hawks rode up slowly, his keen eyes fixed upon her, sitting his horse as imperturbably as any cowboy, and it came over her suddenly that this mesa was his old home, these wild cowboys the only companions he had known. All the ephemeral polish he had picked up in Boston had been sloughed as a snake sheds its skin, and now in chaps and jumper he had taken the color of his surroundings and was as rough and unmanageable as any of them. She even noted, and for the first time, a pistol in his chaps, its ivory handle half concealed behind a flap, and underneath his broad hat his eyes peered out warily as if seeing an enemy even in her.

'You look like a real cowboy,' she said with a half smile. 'Will ... will you be sorry, when I'm gone?'

He shrugged his shoulders and smiled back enigmatically.

'It was Keck,' he said, 'and you know it as well as I do. You've been hypnotized by that unprincipled hound. But I've got too much respect for your mother and you to allow it to go any further. We're going to hook up and start back for Powder Springs, just as soon as you can pack your trunk.'

'I'll never see him again,' she promised impulsively.

'You can't help seeing him,' he insisted, 'if you stay here at the ranch ... and I'll tell you, Penny, I've got some riding to do. You heard about those cattle that the rustlers are stealing...?'

'Oh, are you going out to find them?'

'I've got to,' he said, 'that's what my father sent me out here to do.'

'We'll wait,' she sighed contentedly, 'until you return.'

'I don't think so,' he said, 'I should take you back to town. Be reasonable, Penny, and consider your mother.'

Mrs Pennyman stood waiting with a broom in one hand, an apologetic smile on her flushed face. 'I'll have to confess,' she said, 'the house is thoroughly cleaned, but unfortunately the cook has quit. He resented my sweeping out the kitchen.'

'Oh, then, I can learn to cook!' cried Penny joyously. 'We'll cook for him, won't we, Mother?'

'I had planned to cook for myself, for the few days we're here.'

'But we're going to stay, Mother!' corrected Penny.

'We'll have to talk about that,' Hawks qualified hastily. 'Has the cook gone back to town?'

'No, he's out at the bunkhouse, sulking. It seems it's his regular duty to go out with the cowboys, but, knowing that we were coming, Mister Keck very kindly...'

'I'll send him to the wagon,' said Hawks.

'I think it will be just as well,' she agreed, her eyes twinkling. 'He hasn't a very attractive personality.'

'I didn't like his pancakes,' confided Penny under her breath. 'Don't you think I could learn to make them, Mother?'

'Why, of course, child,' she answered, 'if you'll only give your mind to it. But I will cook for the few days we're here.'

'Now, Mother,' protested Penny, 'why do you always talk that way?'

'I'll have to be going away, Missus Pennyman,' began Hawks apologetically, 'to hunt up those steers that we've lost. If you prefer, I can take you to town first, but if you'd like to stay a few days...?'

'Yes, we'll stay,' sighed Mrs Pennyman, 'until Penny has had her fling. But don't let us keep you, Clayton.'

'He wanted to go right away,' whispered Penny significantly. 'Don't you think we could stay here alone?'

'Why, I suppose so,' she answered dubiously. 'I presume Mister Keck...'

'He won't be back,' Penny cut in hastily.

'Well, really, Clayton,' smiled Mrs. Pennyman, 'I've taken quite a pleasure in cleaning up this dirty old house. I was considered a good housekeeper when I was young. So if it isn't an imposition, I'd like to remain three or four days, if only to finish up what I've begun. Of course, if you and Penny...'

'I told him he could go,' stated Penny. 'I'd just love to live out here ... alone.'

'No, I'll stay,' said Hawks, and, despite their protestations, he lingered on day after day. First he drove into town to bring back supplies for their comfort, then he placed bolts and padlocks on the doors, but all the time he was watching Penny, trying to read what was going on in her mind. All her wild ways had left her. She helped about the house, and rode out with Hawks every day, but always, when he was not looking, she gazed away to the east, where the wagon had disappeared in the distance. And when he was talking, she listened with a smile, but with a faraway look in her eyes. She was dreaming of something else – she did not hear what he was trying to say. And she avoided the touch of his hand. Always before she had been elusive, putting a barrier up between them her lover could never cross by himself, but she herself had moments when she crossed it like a whirlwind and over-whelmed him with passionate kisses. He had never become accustomed to her love-making. But ever since their quarrel she had watched him without seeming to, and, when he reached out his hand, she was gone.

The first week of their visit passed, and

Hawks made no more mention of the task that had brought him to the ranch, but every day he rode farther and farther to the south until, at last, he looked over the rim. There, beneath the brooding sunshine, lay the broad sweep of their winter range, with Look-Out Mountain, a black patch against the sky. The Bear's Ear rose to greet him behind the chalk cliffs of Vermilion Wash where the badlands and 'Dobe town began, but his eyes came to rest on the deep gash of Irish Cañon where the road went through to Coon Hole. His duty lay there, but he must wait.

As the second week began, he assembled his pack outfit and slung a scabbard for his rifle on his saddle, but, although they urged him not to wait, the uneasiness still haunted him, and finally he ventured to speak to Mrs. Pennyman.

'If I go,' he suggested, 'who's going to look after Penny?'

'Why, I will,' said Mrs. Pennyman, surprised.

'Ride out with her everywhere and see that she keeps out of trouble? That's a pretty big contract, Missus Pennyman.'

'No, I can't ride, of course, but Penny has been so obedient ... I can ask her to stay at home while you're gone.'

'She won't do it. She's just waiting for me to leave, I'm afraid, and then she'll go to that wagon.'

'Why, Clayton? What do you mean? And why shouldn't she go?'

'Because,' he declared heatedly, 'I don't trust that man Keck. He's capable of 'most anything with a woman.'

'Well, I must say, Clayton, I think you're entirely unfair in treating Mister Keck as you do. When we met him in town, he seemed a perfect gentleman, and he certainly hasn't intruded. Or have you given him orders not to come to the house as long as my daughter remains?'

'He got his orders from Bones,' answered Hawks.

'And do I understand you to imply that my daughter must be watched to keep her from some affair with Mister Keck?'

Mrs. Pennyman's calm eyes were beginning to blaze, but Hawks kept resolutely on. 'If you knew what I know about your daughter and Mister Keck... '

'There's nothing disgraceful, I hope.'

'No,' he sulked, 'there's nothing disgraceful.'

'Then, I think,' she stated, 'you are going pretty far, and I'm surprised that Penny has submitted to it. I know your father, Clayton Hawks, and you're as alike as two peas, and I must say, if he is jealous, he can be the most unreasonable human being...'

'That's enough,' he said. 'I'll be going.'

'And as far as I'm concerned,' she went on very distinctly, 'Mister Keck is welcome here any time.'

Chapter Six

It was sixty miles to Coon Hole, and Hawks had covered a good ten of it when he reined in his horse with a jerk – he had ridden off without his six-shooter. Since his saddle gun was in the house where Penny and her mother were, he had not even tried to get it; in fact he had forgotten all about it. All he had done was to throw on the pack he had prepared for the trip and spur off without saying good bye – he had forgotten his coffee pot, too.

'Well, you *are* a damned fool,' he burst out vindictively and spurred on again at a high trot. The late encounter with Mrs. Pennyman was merely the culmination of a series of irritating circumstances, not the least of which was the calm assumption of the Pennymans that he had nothing on his mind but them. As a matter of fact he had neglected his own business to putter around the house and ride with Penny, and, if his father learned about it, he would be the most unreasonable human being. So he was jealous, like his father! A pretty good father, too, if he were unreasonable when some woman tried to bend him to her whims, but it was no use for a Hawks to match his will against a Pennyman – they had lost at it, father and son. Mrs. Pennyman had been the unbending maiden who had driven his father to the wilds. Afterward, they had both married someone else.

There was a moral to the story of their warped and tangled destinies if one cared to take the trouble to find it, but his Hawks blood was up, and Hawks put it all from his mind to consider the case of Coon Hole. Here was a problem that he felt perfectly capable of handling, since no women were even remotely involved, and, if the sheriff and two deputies had found their guns insufficient, he wouldn't need his six-shooter, anyway. Probably better off without it – might get him into trouble and give them an excuse to shoot him. He rode up over the rim without looking back and dipped down onto the headwaters of the Alkali. Here, according to Keck, there was a Lazy B line camp, to push their cattle away from the Hole, but look as he would he could find no sign of smoke or tent – or of cattle, for that matter. The wide plain was deserted, not a horse or cow on it, so the line rider had evidently done his duty. Either that or the rustlers had cleaned them out.

The grim lines about Hawks's jaw drew in a little deeper. He spurred faster toward the cedar brakes beyond, and, as the sun was setting, he came out through the foothills onto the flats around Irish Lake. Here under the brow of the jagged range that cut them off from Coon Hole, a bunch of cattle were knee-deep in the blue stem, and, as he rode past them, Hawks saw the swallow-fork in each left ear and knew them for Lazy B cows. So this was the way the line rider pushed them back from the divide – they were bunched up at the very entrance of Irish Cañon! Hawks circled them inquisitively, working nearer to read the brands, and suddenly, as they turned, he spied a fresh-burned brand. It was a Heart brand on a big yearling calf.

He stopped his horse and watched. Then throwing his pack animal loose, he shook out his rope and charged. The cattle scattered before him, heading at a gallop for the cedar brakes, but he caught the yearling on the edge of the brush. It was running with a cow that had a younger calf beside her, but, as the yearling danced and bawled at the end of the rope, the cow turned back and ran to him. She was his mother, and a Lazy B. Her calf was a Lazy B, but the yearling had a freshly seared Heart.

'Something rotten here somewhere,' muttered Hawks, and turned the fighting crea-

63

ture loose. They were across the line, in the State of Colorado, but he had never heard of a Heart brand, even there. Then it came to him – it was Old Man Payne's! This was the work of the Coon Hole cedar-snappers.

'It's about time I came down here,' he grumbled truculently. 'These jaspers have been stealing us blind.'

He rode on down to the lake and watered his horses just at sundown, but after a hasty supper the fever to push on came back on him, and he saddled up and plunged into the cañon. It was a deep gash through the mountains and dark as a pocket. His horses shied at the echoes of their own hoofs, and, as he spurred them unwillingly on, Hawks remembered how in the old days the cattle had been afraid of Irish Cañon. Its reverberating echoes had been considered protection enough to keep them from drifting south into Coon Hole, but perhaps now they had had some rustlers at their tails He had a vision in his mind of eight hundred Lazy B steers being forced down this black and eerie cañon, and then of a sudden he fell to cursing Keck for leaving such a gateway unwatched.

There he was, up on the mesa where the cattle were perfectly safe, range branding in the track of his spring roundup, while down on the lower range, with not a cowboy in sight, yearling mavericks were being stolen and branded with a Heart. And old Bones had had the nerve to defend Keck! He had put up a big fight to keep Hawks from discharging Keck when it was apparent that he was neglecting his duty. Could it be – Hawks stopped, but the thought forced itself upon him – could it be that Bones was standing in with Keck? He had a hard name among the cowboys of the country on account of his penurious ways, and he certainly had stood up for Keck. Right or wrong, he would not hear of Hawks's discharging Keck, and there seemed to be some understanding between them. When Bones was giving his orders and raving his loudest, Keck had sat there and listened to him calmly, and right in the midst of it he had begged to be excused before the cowboys killed someone.

Hawks jabbed the spurs into his horse as it shied and flew back, and cursed the echoes – and Bones. There was, indeed, something wrong here. He even began to doubt whether Old Man Payne was so bad – Bones was evidently prejudiced against him – and Hawks remembered again the peculiar, crooked smile with which Bones had sent him forth on this quest. All he would talk about was Payne and his being a Secessionist, and the tough gang of rustlers he had around him, and, when Hawks had announced that he would go down and get his steers, old Bones had grinned like a cat. Perhaps few tears would be shed by him if

Clayton Hawks should get killed, because then Bones would take over their ranch.

The dark labyrinth of the cañon took on a gloom that was sepulchral. Hawks's horses were in a lather from fright, and after miles of tortuous turnings the huge chasm still stretched before them, echoing and resounding to every hoof clack. It was well along toward midnight when, wrung and exhausted, he fought his way out the lower end, and by then he seriously doubted if, even in broad noonday, a herd of cattle could be forced through that vent. The old-time cowboys had had it right – those echoes were better than a drift fence.

He had come out into a broad and starlit valley, sloping off into mysterious distances on every side, and after rounding an island-like rock he camped against its base, tying his horses to prevent them from bolting. Dawn found them drawn and miserable, chafing irritably at their tie ropes as they strained to reach the grass all about, but he hobbled out only one of them, keeping the other on a rope, for they seemed to sense the presence of some enemy. Seen in daylight, Coon Hole was a beautiful natural park, covered with sagebrush and clumps of verdant cedar. Green meadows lay below them, dotted with horses and cattle, and the mountains to the south were snowcapped. To the east it stretched off endlessly, a level floor of grass and sagebrush, flanked with a rimrock of pine-clad ridges, but the trail led off west, and there, down a swale, Hawks could see the winding willows of a stream. The mountains at the north were rough and covered with cedars, now black in patches like the shadows of angry clouds, now white and barren of brush, and at the west, where they met the line of invisible river, they rose up in a grim, blank wall. That was the effect of it all, of a place shut in and sinister, green and smiling but steeped in evil.

Now that his berserker rage had passed, Hawks began to miss his six-shooter and wonder if he had not been a little rash, but he had come into the rustlers' retreat, and, if he turned back now, it might appear that he was afraid. And if he were found in hiding, or even riding across the valley, he might be mistaken for a detective. According to the etiquette of the country he was due to ride past the Payne Ranch and make himself known at the house. He boiled some coffee in a tomato can and, after letting his horses graze, rode off down the trail to the west. It was a well-traveled trail, and the predominance of shod horse tracks indicated the presence of quite a number of men but, except for cattle and horses and a scourge of mosquitoes, Coon Hole seemed absolutely deserted

As they passed a gushing spring, where the

meadowland began, a horde of deer flies settled down upon his horses, and in spite of their frantic writhing their breasts were soon blooded, while enormous horse flies added further to their misery. Yet the horses that lived here were plump and shiny, despite the constant blood-sucking they endured. Without seeming to notice them Hawks read the horse brands as he passed along, and some of the best were in the Heart iron, but that they were stolen seemed almost certain as they were all vented from other brands, most of which were unknown in these parts. Some Montana brands he knew, and there were others that he had heard of as coming from Colorado and Utah, but, as he rode past a herd of cattle, he saw the Heart brand on two big steers, old brands that had long ago peeled. He reined in his horse to make absolutely certain and rode off down the trail. Whoever owned that brand was stealing his cattle, and who could it be but Payne?

The valley pinched in until it was less than a mile wide, with a bluff on the farther side, and, as the formation changed from blood-red sandstone to white lime, a series of springs burst forth. A round corral, for breaking horses, appeared on the flat, and a horseman galloped off up a draw. As Hawks rounded the point, he came suddenly upon the ranch house, tucked away in a pocket of the hills. It was a long log cabin, with a spring house and cold cellar, and stables and pole corrals out behind, but the thing he noticed most as he rode up toward the gate was a row of flaunting hollyhocks, standing along the front yard fence. Somehow they did not fit in with his preconceived notions of what a rustlers' hide-out was like.

A dog rushed out, furiously barking and leaping against the gate, and a man glanced out the door, then, as he stepped out deliberately, the doorway behind him was filled with staring faces. Hawks barely noticed them, except that two were women's and the third was that of a tough-looking boy. The old man who stood before him commanded all his attention, besides making his heart miss a beat. He was tall and white-bearded with a high, war-eagle nose and eyes as fiercely penetrating as an Indian's. After a long look at Hawks, and a longer one at his horse brands, he spoke to the raving dog.

'Good morning,' greeted Hawks as the dog was quieted. 'I was looking for that trail that goes south. Can you tell me where it cuts through the rim?'

'There is no such trail,' the old man stated distinctly, and waited for Hawks to call him a liar.

'Can't you get through south at all?'

'No, sir,' replied Payne. 'You cannot.'

Hawks shrugged his shoulders and said

nothing. Perhaps Bones was correct in his estimate of Telford Payne. 'All right,' he said, and reined his horse away. But the moment the conversation had started, the woman in the doorway had stepped out, and at each question and answer she edged a little nearer until now she stood beside her husband. She was a big, handsome woman in the full prime of life, and her eyes had been fixed on Hawks with a careful appraisal that he felt was not missing a point. His boots, his hat, his chaps, and cowboy's jumper, his pack and the brand on his horse all had undergone a minute inspection, and now she turned her eyes on him. They were large brown eyes, showing too much of the whites, and, as he reined away, she spoke.

'Are you working for Bones?' she asked.

'No ma'am,' he said a trifle defiantly.

'You're riding a Lazy B horse,' she said. 'Oh ... maybe you're riding for Keck?'

'Nope. I'm riding for myself.'

'What? You aren't that Mister Hawks that has just come back from the East and is staying up at the Lazy B Ranch?'

'That's my name,' he admitted. 'Well, good day.'

He started off once again, but she halted him once more.

'What's your business down here?' she demanded.

'Oh, just riding through,' he said. 'Down

70

looking for some cattle and horses.'

'Did you find them?' she flashed back.

'Not yet.'

'I suppose,' she taunted, as her husband turned away, 'you think we stole them?'

'I don't think anything,' he answered. 'Just looking around. And by the way, who runs this Heart brand?'

Her eyes opened up wider as he fired this Parthian shot, and she turned to glance at her husband, but he, as if intolerant of her woman's tongue, had gone back into the house. In his place now stood his son, a lanky, hatchet-faced boy, and girl even more handsome than her mother, but in spite of her buxom figure and the doll-like beauty of her face Hawks did not respond to her coquettish smile. It reminded him somehow of Penny.

'The Heart brand?' repeated Mrs Payne. 'I don't believe I ever heard of it. Our brand is TP united.'

'Yes ... all right,' he nodded, determined not to be drawn into a controversy, but the lady had not finished with him yet.

'I'm Missus Payne,' she smiled. 'We've been down here two years. How does Miss Penny like the country out here?'

'Very much,' he answered formally. 'If you're coming by our way, I'm sure she'd be glad to have you call.'

She blinked and looked at him sharply, to

make sure there was no mistake, and then a rosy blush suffused her face, for they had not even asked him to dismount. 'Get down,' she invited. 'I thought you were some detective that old Bones had sent down to insult us. Charley, go out and help him tie his horses.'

'Well ... thanks,' Hawks responded. 'I won't come in. But I would like a drink of cold water.'

He swung down from his horse and stepped inside the gate, and again the row of hollyhocks caught his eye. They were protected from within by an ornamental fence made of cedar posts wattled with willow twigs, and up toward the spring house there was an old-fashioned garden, full of verbenas and petunias and pansies. His opinion of Mrs. Payne suddenly rose, although she had lied about the brand, but a woman who loved flowers enough to raise them in Coon Hole was far from being abandoned. He noted, also, that she wore a freshly ironed house dress that brought out the trim lines of her figure, and the mass of soft brown hair coiled about her shapely head gave an added effect of neatness. There was an air of grace and of breeding about both herself and her daughter, but Payne made a very churlish host. He had remained inside the cabin, and Mrs. Payne had seemed relieved when Hawks merely asked for a drink.

'Come out to the spring house,' she said.

'So you're not working for Bones? Mister Payne is so enraged at the way Bones has been sending officers down here that he can hardly be civil to anyone. I don't doubt Bones told you some story about our stealing his cows ... and he's always sending officers down to search ... and yet his Forty-Four cowboys have stole more of our calves than he has had losses. What he's trying to do is run us out of the Hole so he can have it for his winter range. But Mister Payne won't be intimidated, that's all.'

'You have a very pretty garden,' spoke up Hawks admiringly. 'I don't know when I've seen one more beautiful. And these wildflowers, here ... the sego lilies and columbines ... I suppose they've been transplanted from the hills?'

'Yes, they're transplanted,' she answered, 'but Mary does that. I think it's all foolishness myself, with vegetables and garden truck so scarce.'

'Oh, then it isn't the young lady that I met at the gate?'

'No, that's Pearl. Mary is younger, but she's shy. Oh, dear, somebody has carried off that cup!'

She started back impatiently toward the house, and Hawks looked at the garden again. He was turning away when there was a rustle among the clematis, and Mary stepped out of her hiding place. She was like a flower herself with her golden hair and shy blue eyes, and, as he met her gaze, she picked the tallest columbine and pressed it into his hands with a smile.

Chapter Seven

From a man named Bones and engaged in the cow business, one would expect little of poetry or sentiment, but Hawks wondered as he rode away why some mention had not been made of the family of Telford Payne. The fact that he was a cow thief had been repeated and made much of, and the fact that he was the head of a tough gang but Mrs. Payne and her two daughters might never have existed, as far as Bones was concerned. Hawks had expected Payne to be about what he was, a surly, misanthropic old man, but he had certainly not expected him to keep a wife and family at the hold-out of a gang of rustlers. Women and children do not belong in a social formation of that kind, and especially girls like Mary Payne.

She was shy, of course, and after giving him the flower she had retreated around the corner of the spring house, but he could see at a glance that she was like her dainty col-

74

umbines, transplanted from a happier clime. In the sordid surroundings of Coon Hole she had planted this garden in response to something fine within her, and Clay treasured in his jumper the flower she had given him. Such things happen now and then to the grimmest of men engaged on the grimmest of errands, just as chance flowers look up from the wayside, but as he jogged off down the wash, Clay wondered about her life there and what would be her ultimate fate.

He had expected, when he rode up, to find Payne's house full of rustlers, foul-mouthed and more than ready to start a fight, but the rustlers, if there were any, were conspicuous by their absence, although the shod horse tracks still continued as he went west. What kind of a dog's trick was Bones trying to play on him when he represented this as a hell hole of iniquity? Mrs Payne had come close to expressing what he himself had in mind when she claimed that old Bones was trying to oust them, but still Coon Hole must have its rustlers because some man, he knew, had branded his yearling calf with a Heart. All the rest might be moonshine and malicious exaggeration, to stir up adverse sentiment against the Paynes, but eight hundred head of steers had disappeared around there somewhere, and one calf had been branded out of his iron.

The trail that he was following brought him

in sight of a rich river bottom with a forest of bright green cottonwoods, but, turning to the south, the trail kept well away from it, crossing the creek and mounting a long ridge. Once more the river appeared, and, as he circled a high point, he beheld it in all its beauty. In great, lazy curves it threaded its way among the cottonwoods toward the mouth of a shadowy cañon, and there it was swallowed up as if the earth had engulfed it or the mountains sucked it into their maw. Cliffs three thousand feet high marked the beginning of its passage, and for hundreds of miles it crept through sunless chasms on its way to the Grand Cañon of the Colorado.

Surely where the river barred the way there could be no Robbers' Trail, nor yet down the boxed-in cañon, and the mountains through which it cut were so rugged and steep that a trail to the south seemed impossible. But Bones had insisted, and others had borne him out, that the rustlers had a trail leading south, and, since the shod tracks still led on, Hawks spurred down the bank to the edge of the silent stream. At the first melting of snows it had overflowed its banks, filling the lagoons that lay behind the numerous sand-bars, and even yet the green water boiled and sucked in treacherous whirlpools that made crossing it out of the question. The trail struck into mud and quicksand, and, as he passed through the willows, the mosquitoes gathered about them in clouds. Assailed from every side his animals thrashed and fought their heads until he was glad to let them run away, and, when they had gained the windy summit of the bluff, Hawks gave up and turned back east.

The high mountains of the rim rose like a wall before him as he rode along through a wilderness of sage, and after skirting it for ten miles he turned north on some old cow tracks that seemed to lead down from his range. Coon Hole lay below him at the base of the black mountain – he had circled almost completely around it – but these tracks seemed to come from the mouth of Vermilion Cañon, where Vermilion Wash broke through the barrier of the hills. He spurred forward through the cedars, and suddenly the steer-tracks thickened, all coming from the cañon and heading south, but, as he swung around the point that barred the mouth of the cañon, he stopped short and sniffed the air. On the wind that sucked down through the dark chasm before him he caught the tang of smoke.

Visions of campfires and hard-eyed rustlers rose up before his eyes as he dropped off and crept forward through the rocks, but the cañon mouth was deserted – even the smell of smoke was gone – and, at last, he returned to his horse. In the days when he had ridden the range Vermilion Cañon was impassable on account of the quicksands and waterfalls, but if those cattle had been driven through, it was time that he knew about it, because others must have gone through before. The mystery of the lost steers was a mystery no longer if he could believe the story of these tracks. Here was the hole that Bones was raving about, the leak that must be stopped, the secret of eight hundred lost steers. He mounted and rode in slowly, scanning the shelves of the shattered cliffs, keeping a wary eye ahead, but, although his horses snorted and snuffed the wind, the gloomy cañon was deserted.

A brawling stream of water, milky with alkali from the badlands, flowed down over the sandstone reefs, and soon, as the cañon pinched in, it occupied the whole creekbed except for the narrow margin cleared by floods. Above the portals of the gateway the streambed became more level, with quicksand between the low waterfalls, but the cattle had found it passable, and Hawks spurred his frightened horse until he plunged from one bog hole to another. The pack horse, tied head to tail, pulled back and didn't want to follow, but Hawks forced him up ledges breast high until, at last, muddy and swearing, he stood below a waterfall that he knew could never be sealed. Vermilion Cañon was passable, but only one way, for this jump-off was ten feet high, and in the quicksand at its base he saw the tips of cedar limbs that had been thrown in to support the leaping steers. They had been rushed through pell-mell, across quicksands and over water-falls, but Hawks would have to back out.

The long day was nearing its close when Hawks came out into the open, and, as he turned to look to the rear, he thought he heard his own name shouted out above the brawling of the stream. He looked up and down the cañon, then up at the high cliffs, and his name was called again.

'Hello, Clay!'

He searched the side of the cliff from which the sound had come and caught a sudden movement among the rocks. High up among the ledges a face stared out of a crevice, a face as wild and ferocious as a caveman's, but, as he gazed at it, dumbfounded, the man burst into laughter as familiar as the face was alien; It was a white face, ghastly white, half covered with a bristling beard, and hair as black and thick as an Indian's.

'Hello!' responded Hawks, 'who are you, anyway?'

'It's Rooster!' laughed the caveman. 'Rooster Raslem!'

There was a minute of dead silence as Hawks stared at him doubtfully, and then he threw up his hand. 'Hello, Rooster, old boy!' he shouted joyfully. 'Come on down! I'm glad to see you!'

The caveman hesitated, reached back into his cavern, and came down, carrying a gun. As he stepped from rock to rock, he paused warily, like a squirrel, fixing Hawks with beady black eyes, but when he reached the stony slope that extended down to the streambed, he straightened up with a jovial grin. He was a short man but quick and active as a chipmunk, and, as he looked at Hawks, he cocked his head to one side in the movement that had given him his name.

'Seen you go up,' he explained, and the grin suddenly vanished as Hawks stepped down from his horse. Quick as a flash the rifle leaped up to his hip, only to drop back again as Hawks smiled.

'Well, well,' exclaimed Hawks, 'you're the first man I asked for when I got back home last week!'

''S that so,' murmured Rooster. 'I suppose you heard?'

'Yes, I heard,' returned Hawks, now suddenly grave, 'but I wouldn't believe it until Bones showed me the advertisement.'

'Five thousand dollars reward, eh?' suggested Rooster.

'That's what it said, but I don't believe it yet. I've known you too well, Rooster ... you wouldn't do a thing like that ... but it sure got me in wrong with old Bones. I'm not so stuck on this wagon boss he's got ... he was drunk when I was in town ... but when I put

80

up a talk to have him fired, Bones asked who I could get that was any better. "Why, Rooster!" I said, and when I'd put myself on record, he pulled this sheriff's circular and gave me the horse laugh. I told him I *knew* you were honest.'

Rooster smiled, a trifle sadly, and shuffled his feet. 'You're the first man I've talked to,' he said. And then, after a silence, he spoke up defiantly: 'I suppose I can trust you, Clay? I'm worth five thousand dollars, you know, to any man that will turn me up, and...'

'Don't you worry,' nodded Hawks, 'you're safe. I don't need the money that bad.'

'Well, gimme a smoke, then,' begged Raslem. He accepted the makings, rolled a cigarette, and inhaled luxuriously, cocking his head as he looked up at Hawks. 'I was expecting you'd come back,' he said.

'About time,' observed Hawks. 'They're stealing us blind. Been bringing 'em down through here, I reckon.' He glanced knowingly at Raslem who feigned not to hear him.

'I was dying for a smoke,' he puffed, 'or I'd never've showed my head. Let you go up, all right, but when you came back ... say, is this all the makings you've got?'

Hawks turned to his pack and threw off the lashings. 'How're you fixed for grub?' he asked.

'Bum,' grumbled Raslem. 'Been living on straight beef for two weeks.'

Hawks opened up his pack sacks and measured out some coffee and bacon, emptying the rest of his provisions into a bag. 'I'll be home by tomorrow noon,' he explained.

'Is that all for me?' spoke up Raslem, and, when Hawks nodded, he held out his hand. 'You're all right, Clay,' he said. 'Come on up to the cave... I'm dying to have a talk.'

Chapter Eight

A sudden animation had come over Rooster Raslem. He seemed to caper as he bounded up to his cave, and, sticking his head out, he laughed long and loud as Hawks stumbled after him with the bag. 'How's this for a hold-out?' he shouted boastfully. 'Ever look for a man up here? I been here three months, holed up like a rabbit ... any detective come by your place? Well, they did, all right, only you won't recognize 'em. They're hunting for me everywhere. Must be some around here, because the man that brings me grub ain't showed up for more than a month. Come in! What do you think of my cave?'

He stepped back from the narrow cleft that

served him for an entrance and jerked his head sideways, like a rooster. It was a nervous trick he had – mentioned in detail in the sheriff's circular along with the fact that he was a great talker – and Hawks smiled at the memories it conjured. In the old days, when he had been a cowboy, learning his job with the rest, Raslem had been his *fidus* Achates, his partner in many a wild prank – and he was the old Rooster, still. He was short and bowlegged, with a disproportionately long body, looking in fact like a very tall cowboy who had been driven into the ground about a foot. And his eyes were dancing with mischief as he exhibited his hiding place.

It was no more than a long cleft behind a great shoulder of rock that had parted from the cliff above, and, by walling up one end and making a stairway up to the other, he had converted it into a living place, a narrow cell about twenty feet long. The overhang of the stratum above made a roof in all weather, there was a crack that led off most of his smoke, and close by the fireplace he had constructed a crude bed out of cedar poles strung with rawhide. A quarter of beef hung back in a cranny, two pistols in a cartridge belt adorned the wall, and in the soot above the fireplace there were curious faces and figures, scratched one on top of the other.

'Pretty good!' praised Hawks, taking in every detail and coming back to the faces on the wall. 'What's this here ... some cliff-dwelling stuff?'

'That's my blackboard,' laughed Raslem. 'Got to pass the time somehow, so I make up all these pictures on the wall. Don't that show some class?' He pointed to a portrait, limned with charcoal on the gray wall – a portrait composed entirely of letters. 'Make it out?' he challenged. 'Come on, now, you're so smart ... what word do them letters make?'

Hawks looked at it closer, admiring its ingenuity but not discovering the particular word at first glance An E formed the mouth, an L the nose, an A the eye, an S the ear, and for the forehead an R, for the chin an M, with a half moon for the head and hair.

'Read 'em off,' prompted Raslem. 'Here, begin at the top, then skip to the eye and ear. R-A-S-L-E-M! Gee willikens, boy, what did they learn you in school?'

'It's your signature, eh?' said Hawks, 'a kind of monogram.'

'Sure. It's my moniker ... my high sign. When the Wild Bunch sees that, they'll understand.'

'Pretty smooth,' conceded Hawks, 'but at the same time, Rooster, I don't like to see you in with that bunch. This train-robbing business doesn't pay.'

'The hell it don't,' came back Rooster. 'I'd just like to show you my roll ... it comes close to ten thousand dollars. What do you want me to do ... punch cows all my life for a stinking little dollar a day? Another day, another dollar. A million days, a million dollars. Will a man ever get rich at that?'

'No,' replied Hawks, 'but he'll keep out of the penitentiary ... and you don't have to punch cows all your life. If you'd kept out of this racket, you'd be my wagon boss right now.'

'Too late, now, to talk about that.' Raslem turned to the fireplace and threw on some kindling, but, as he nursed the sulky fire, he was thinking. 'This country has gone to hell!' he burst out angrily. 'They don't give a poor man a chance. You don't realize, Clay, what a change has come over things since you and your old man went East. He kind of held the bunch down and put the fear of God in their hearts, but now... Christ! ... what's the use? There's old Bones over on Snake River, feeding his 'punchers on sowbelly and working 'em from daylight to dark ... and then this cheap sport Keck that he promoted at the Lazy B ... didn't he fire every one of the old gang? And look at the bunch of Texans he's working up there now ... they'd cut a man's throat for a nickel!'

'I believe it,' answered Hawks, 'but what's that got to do with holding up trains? No, I tell you, Rooster...'

'It's got a lot to do with it!' Raslem broke in vehemently. 'You don't know what I've been up against, Clay. You hadn't been gone a month when this man Keck began to pick on me, and to work the boss to hire more Texans. Inside of six months, all the old boys had quit and the *Tejanos* were manning the outfit. Then they began to ride old Butterfield until he gave up and quit, and Bones made Keck wagon boss. No chance for me then with the Lazy Bs, so I went over and took on with Bones ... down on the river with the Forty-Fours. Working from daylight to dark and stand guard two hours every night, and nothing but sowbelly and beans! And only paid me thirty a month. Your old man paid me forty, and I earned every nickel of it, but Bones beat me down to thirty.'

Raslem piled on more wood and opened two cans of corn, raking some coals out to fry his strips of bacon.

'No corrals,' he went on querulously, 'and no pastures to hold our horses. If we'd ask him for a nighthawk to take care of the cavvy, he'd swear we were making him bankrupt. But it was the grub, more than anything ... nothing but sowbelly ... sowbelly and beef all around us ... too damned stingy to let us kill a yearling stray. Well, we were down on Snake River, and he'd gone back for some stamp irons when I jumped a big deer, right down there by the crossing, and roped him before he could get into the brush. We drug him to the wagon, and I killed him with my six-

86

shooter, and old Charley, the cook, had both frying pans working when Bones rode up, boiling mad.

'"Who killed that beef?" he hollered. "God damn you cussed cowboys, you break their legs on purpose! Who killed that beef, I say?"'

'He seen the meat hanging up and naturally thought it was a yearling, and we was all too bowled over to tell him. So we let him yammer a while, and then I got up ... I was hot. "Mister Bones," I says, "that ain't no beef."'

'"Whoa! Whoa!" he says as his horse shied at the carcass and damned nigh throwed him off, "stand still, you fool."'

'Well, his horse wasn't bucking, nor anything like it, but he's a mean old jasper, and he was ringy by that time, so he made a swipe at its head with a stamp iron. The old son-of-a-bitch... I jerked out my six-shooter and pointed it right at his belly.'

'"You drop that iron!" I said. "You hit that horse again, and I'll have you rolling snowballs in hell."'

'He knowed I meant it, too, because I won't see no horse abused, and this was nothing but a half-broke colt. But it stuck in his craw to see us eating that meat, and he still thought we'd killed a beef. 'Course, we used to cripple 'em on purpose, sometimes.'

'"Who killed that beef?" he says, gitting

down off of his horse, and by that time I could fight a buzz saw.

"'I did!" I says, "only it ain't got your brand, so you don't need to holler."

"'Now, here, gentlemen," says old Charley ... you know how polite he always was ... "what's the use of all this fussing over nothing? This ain't no steer, Mister Bones. This is nothing but a deer that Rooster roped and killed with his six-shooter."

'Well, old Bones had to take water and acknowledge he was wrong, but he gave me my time the next day. Said a man with my temper was liable to make trouble, and he didn't care to have me around. So there I was ... fired and winter coming on ... nothing to do but get out and ride the chuck line ... so I says to hell with being respectable and came over and joined the 'Dobe Town gang.'

'Been doing fine ever since, eh?' suggested Hawks.

'Fine as frog's hair,' asserted Raslem. 'Never regretted it for a minute. But old Bones is the man that drove me to it. I'll get his scalp before I reform.'

'Oh, reform, eh?' laughed Hawks. 'So *you're* going to reform, too? But, I suppose, like all the rest you're going to pull off one more job...'

'Two more,' said Raslem briskly, 'and I quit!'

Hawks looked at him a minute and

changed the subject abruptly – he knew that Raslem meant every word of it, and he was a man who could be pressed only so far. Besides, the die was cast, the Pinkertons were on his trail, and there was five thousand dollars reward on his head. He was a hunted man, a fugitive from justice – and he had taken the belt and six-shooters from the wall. They lay on the bed, close at hand while he was cooking, and Hawks understood what that meant. Like his enemy, Bones, Raslem had adopted the motto: Don't tempt any man too far and don't trust any man too far. Three months of solitude had made him jumpy. Yet he was glad, ever so glad, to have company.

'Out hunting cows?' he asked with a mischievous twinkle. 'Thought I saw you looking down at them tracks.'

'Yes, and I'll find where they went to,' Hawks answered, 'before I'm many days older. Bones tried to tell me that it was the Payne outfit down here that was running off all our steers...'

'Old Bones,' stated Raslem with much profane emphasis, 'is nothing but a cow thief himself.'

'Very likely,' acknowledged Hawks, 'but at the same time I'd like to know who's running this Heart brand in Coon Hole. Missus Payne tried to tell me she'd never heard of it, and the old man called me a liar twice.'

'Now, here,' broke in Raslem, 'don't you jump at conclusions... Payne is a mighty nice man. He may be kind of short with you, if he thinks you're some detective, but he's all right, and his folks are all right. I've stayed down there, and I ought to know.'

'Maybe so. I don't dispute it, but he's got a very unfortunate way with him when it comes to receiving strangers. And who owns that Heart brand, if he doesn't?'

'Hey! Now listen!' cried Raslem aggressively. 'You want to know who runs that brand? Well, you go right back to William Bones and ask *him* who owns it! The Paynes have got nothing to do with it!'

'All right,' shrugged Hawks, 'you ought to know what you're talking about. Come on, let's have something to eat.'

They ate, Raslem prodigiously, Hawks sparingly and mostly beef, not to cut down Raslem's dwindling board, but all the time in the back of his mind Hawks was thinking about the Heart brand. Raslem knew who owned it, knew who was running off his cows, had seen them pass in the cañon below him, but Rooster was an outlaw now and dependent on other outlaws for favors. Their friendship meant more to him than Hawks's. Yet, here for the second time that same hint had cropped up, a hint that Bones was playing him false. But Bones was at war with Payne and all the Coon Hole cedar-snappers, and the Heart cattle were running on Payne's range.

'Well, I'll be going,' said Hawks as soon as he had finished, 'and any time you run out of meat, Rooster, you're welcome to a Lazy B.'

'No! Sit down,' insisted Raslem. 'What's your sweat, all at once? I ain't talked to a man for a month. And speaking of Lazy B beef, I reckon you think you've been eating some, but that's another time when you guessed wrong. I'll travel ten miles any time to get one of Bones's Forty-Fours when there's Lazy Bs right up the cañon. No, sir, Clay, I never steal from my friends.'

'Well, you're welcome,' repeated Hawks. 'It isn't stealing from me, because I've told you to take what you need. And when a man loses eight hundred three and four-year-old steers, he don't mind a calf, now and then.'

He rose to go, but Raslem forced him back in his seat. 'Sit down, dammit,' he cursed, 'and let me give you a tip. Don't you leave the ranch again without your six-shooter. You don't know what chances you're taking.'

'What, with the Payne outfit?'

'Aw, no. What's a-biting you, anyway? Did Bones fill you up with that bunk? Well, you stay with me a while, and I'll tell you more about your own business than you'll find out in a month. What's the use of hurrying off?'

'It's this way,' stated Hawks. 'I know how you're probably fixed, and I don't want to pry into your business. You're dependent upon Payne and that bunch of rustlers he's got down there, and I don't expect you to say a word against them. But if I sit around and chat and get to asking leading questions, you're liable to get the idea I'm snooping.'

'Nothing of the kind,' declared Raslem, pressing him back onto the bed and hanging the belt of six-shooters on the wall. 'I know I can trust you, Clay. Otherwise, I'd either shoot you, right here and now, or pull my freight the minute you're gone. But I'm trusting you, Clay ... a man has got to talk to somebody or go crazy. You're the first human being that I've spoken a word to since me and Sundance Thorp held up that train. Old Payne, nor nobody, don't know where I'm hiding ... they all think I'm in some cave, up in 'Dobe Town ... but now you know where I am, I'm going to ask you as a favor to bring me down a little tobacco. That ain't asking too much, is it? And in return for this favor I'm going to tell you something important.' He jerked his head sideways and gazed at Hawks impressively. 'Look out for that man Keck.'

'All right,' agreed Hawks, 'and then what?'

'Well, do *that!*' burst out Raslem impatiently. 'For Christ's sake, coming off without your six-shooter!'

'Do you mean he might shoot me?'

'Why, that son-of-a-bitch...,' began Raslem, and then he choked with rage. 'Look out for him,' he warned. 'He's a bad one.'

'I know that. I plan to fire him, when I get back.'

'Don't you do it!' urged Raslem. 'He'll kill you, sure as hell. Aw, here, you don't know what's going on.' He grabbed a brand out of the fire and drew a Lazy B on the wall. 'Now, look,' he said, 'that's your cow brand, ain't it? Well, he's burning that into a Heart.'

'Who ... Keck?'

'Surest thing! And he's got two line riders, up here on the Vermilion, pushing the burned stuff down this cañon into Coon Hole.'

'Why, the thieving bastard,' cursed Hawks. 'He's got those men on our payroll.'

'Sure, and *he's* on your payroll,' exulted Raslem. 'Old Bones is on your payroll, too, ain't he?'

'But here,' contended Hawks, his eye back on the brand, 'how can you burn a Lazy B into a Heart? There's that bar ... what becomes of the bar?'

Raslem seized another firebrand and extended the wings of the B until they joined in the tip of the Heart – except for the bar it was perfect. Then he wiped out the Bar and left a Heart. 'That bar is only a hair brand,' he smirked. 'As soon as they shed their hair, the bar is gone ... then they drive 'em off and alter 'em to the Heart.'

'Yes, but who makes the hair brand?' persisted Hawks. 'And those cattle that we lost were big steers.'

'That's just what I'm getting to,' returned Raslem. 'I want to show you what a bunch of crooks they are. When old Bones bought those steers for your father, he sent Keck and them Texans to receive them ... it was somewhere over in Utah ... and, when they branded that stuff, they ran a hair brand on the Bar and altered it to a Heart when they got home. On your own range, mind ye, and working on *your* own time ... now tell me that Bones ain't a crook.'

'Well, if he isn't,' pronounced Hawks, 'he's a damned poor cowman. Didn't anybody ever catch on?'

'*I* did,' asserted Raslem, 'so there must have been others. But you understand now why Keck fired all the old-timers ... he was afraid some honest guys would buck him ... wouldn't allow us around there, and, if any reps came in to the roundup, he put 'em to holding the herd. He and his Texans branded every calf and then, when they shed, they rebranded 'em. Now you know who owns this Heart brand ... it's your own wagon boss ... Keck.'

Hawks nodded his head but remained

silent. Raslem had only begun.

'What d'ye think of Telford Payne now? Willing to admit you might've been wrong? Why, that old feller is a Southern gentleman. He wouldn't dirty his hands by stealing. I'm from Missouri myself, so we're pretty good neighbors, but he's having a hard time, Clay. Just came in and got nicely settled when they punched that Robbers' Trail through ... runs from Canada to the Mexican line ... and now, in spite of hell, he's running a regular hold-out for all the rough characters in the country. They come there, you understand, and he has to take 'em in ... if he didn't, they'd move in anyway ... and then, when they go, they slap his iron on a few horses or leave a bunch of steers on his pasture. He owes money at the bank, so he can't move out, and old Bones is making him trouble all the time. On top of that, Clay, it's a bad place for his womenfolks ... a damned hard place to keep straight.'

'You mean ... his wife?' ventured Hawks, remembering a look in her eyes.

'Yes, and ... well, if Payne knowed what I know, there's one man would sure get his, right square where his suspenders cross. They say now he's making up to Pearl.'

'No,' exclaimed Hawks, 'why, she's only a child!'

'*He* don't care ... he's sure hell for women. They all know his reputation, but that don't

95

make no difference. He goes in to win, and he wins. But here's the damnedest thing ... you'd hardly believe it ... he carries around a scalp lock of their hair.'

Hawks's eyes opened wider, but he put the thought away from him. 'I don't believe it. He'd get killed.'

'It's a fact!' stated Raslem, jerking his hand impressively. 'I've seen it ... a big, long braid. He shows it around when he's drunk. And he carries some little scissors... I've seen them, too ... that he uses to cut off their hair. Carries them around in his vest pocket, and, when he's stole the lock of hair, he plaits it into his braid. Ever hear of anything ranker than that?'

'Don't talk about it,' shuddered Hawks. 'It makes me sick.'

'He ought to be shot,' declared Raslem; 'And you ought to see the cosmetics he keeps. He's got more kinds of lotions, and hair oils, and perfumery ... and he wears gloves, all the time, to keep his hands white.'

'Gloves,' cried Hawks, suddenly leaping to his feet. 'Why, you don't mean...?'

'Sure,' nodded Raslem. 'You know who I mean. Your own wagon boss ... Keck.'

Chapter Nine

The first gleam of day found Hawks in the badlands, spurring north with one of Raslem's pistols in his chaps. For Raslem had had his way. Hawks had avoided the beaten paths, circling wide to throw his enemies off his trail. It was a different world now from the one of two days before when he had started for Coon Hole without his six-shooter. Raslem had peopled it with rustlers, looking down from wooded peaks, watching passes, riding hard to cut him off. And to prove that he meant it Raslem had given him a six-gun from the belt that hung on the wall. After that, there was no room for doubt.

'Ride east,' Raslem had said, 'and make your own trail ... and keep your eye on the rim.'

Twenty miles lay behind Hawks, and now he was headed north across the powdery flats of the badlands. Chalky buttes rose all about him, table-topped and bare of shrubs. The rim ran like a line on either side, and, as he went down into the sink, the line of cliffs seemed to rise until he found himself in 'Dobe Town. Mighty domes and cathedral spires loomed up against the skyline as if built brick by brick by aspiring men, but, since God had done the work, the men who came there to hide had mocked it by calling it 'Dobe Town. Grotesque forms like Silurian monsters raised their heads from eroded points. There were amphitheaters and fluted columns and Corinthian capitols, and deep under the façades of what might pass for Grecian temples ran the caverns that had made 'Dobe Town such a city of refuge.

But it was as a hold-out for outlaws, rather than a refuge for fugitives, that 'Dobe Town had latterly been known, and, as Hawks made his way through it, he kept his eyes on the rim as Rooster Raslem had enjoined him. The solemn silence of this sunken valley, unbroken except for the crunches of his horses' hoofs as they broke through the crust of the alkali, had a sinister significance now, but it came mostly from his own thoughts, which were of Keck and Penny, for he rode out of the badlands in safety. Up the old Rustler's Trail that he had known since boyhood he mounted to the edge of Hawks Mesa, and, when he crept up and looked over the rim, he saw the Lazy B wagon below him.

Uncle Simmy, the cook, was chopping at a log, and, as his axe came back, the sound of the blow reached Hawks, as if he were knocking on air. He ceased, and two more blows came up from the stillness, like echoes out of the past. Here and there across the basin

98

Hawks could see the cattle in motion, disturbed by Keck's cowboys who were range branding. Except for Raslem's warning he would have ridden down among them – he was tempted to do so still. But far into the night the garrulous Rooster Raslem had inveighed against them, describing their giant scheme to defraud him. The winter before, when Green River had become frozen, they had crossed two hundred steers on the ice, and now, back in the cedar brakes, they were holding still others until the river should freeze again. Over in Utah they had confederates who had sold their first cattle – this was the source of the money they were squandering – and the rustlers who made Coon Hole their headquarters looked to Keck for leadership in everything. Did Hawks think they would let one man stand in their way?

A restless impatience urged him to ride down the slope and dash across the mesa to the ranch – there was no water in 'Dobe Town, and his horses were fretting, he himself was hungry and thirsty – but those long hours in the cave, with Rooster Raslem straddling in front of him pouring out curses against Keck and Bones, had put a new fear into his heart. He lay behind the rimrock and watched. The sun was sinking low when the cowboys rode back to the wagon, coming in by ones and twos, but Keck was not among them. Hawks's heart began to thump as the self-accusations of the morning came back with redoubled force. Was all well with Penny? Had he done right to leave her, even with her mother to preach much needed restraint? Was it possible that a perfumed dandy in two weeks' time could woo Charlotte Pennyman and win her? He shuddered as he had shuddered before – she had talked so much of being free.

As the dusk settled in the huge bowl, obscuring the wagon from sight, he mounted and rode down to the water, and then, spurring angrily, he took the trail for the ranch house, regardless of Raslem's solemn warnings. Now that he found himself in action all his pent-up feelings were released, and he cursed the self-sufficiency of the Pennymans. At the bottom of it all lay the complacency of Mrs. Pennyman, her placid taking it for granted that all was well. She did not approve of his objections to Keck's presence. As far as she was concerned, Keck was welcome at any time, and yet here was a man who kept a scalp lock to record his conquests, who hunted women as an Indian hunts deer.

It was dark when he arrived within sight of the ranch house, and he circled it before he rode in. There in the stable was Keck's horse, eating hay as if he lived there, with his saddle flung over the rack. Hawks unsaddled in the horse lot and turned his animals out into the pasture, then crept up to his own house like a thief. There was a light in the kitchen, and, as he looked in through the window, he saw Penny talking quietly with Keck. Mrs Pennyman sat apart, nursing her rheumatism by the warm stove but looking on with a placid smile, and anger swept Hawks like a storm blast.

Here he was, hungry and tired, the night air was chill, all the food and warmth were inside, and yet he must wait till this visit was over or break in and create a scene. With Raslem's pistol beneath his waistband and hunger gnawing at his belly he dared not trust himself too far, for at a word from Keck his hand would leap to his gun, and he would kill him – knowing his heart as he did. He retreated into the darkness and waited. Hour after hour he paced to and fro, sighing wearily as he listened to the laughter, and, when at last Keck arose to go, the Great Dipper was down below the horizon. It was midnight and bitterly cold. Hawks's anger died within him; all he wished for was to end his long misery. The door opened, and Keck stepped forth, followed quickly by the form of Penny, and then as the door closed Hawks saw her leap into his arms and cling there, locked in a kiss.

At daylight he opened the door and started a

fire in the stove, pottering about with trembling hands, and, as nobody stirred, he cooked and ate a hasty breakfast, still pondering what he should say. After the revelation of that kiss there was nothing to do but see Penny and demand back his ring. Although she was in the wrong, he still dreaded that something in her which made her as unconquerable as fate. She would have her own way, in spite of him. Yet come what would, he dared not think of yielding – she must leave the ranch forever. It was necessary to save her from this madness. He was aroused from his meditations by a patter of feet, and Penny slipped through the door.

'Oh! It's *you!*' she cried, and the smile on her lips suddenly froze to something less radiant. 'When did you get home?' she asked demurely.

'Last night,' he stated, 'about nine o'clock. Who did you think it was?' he wondered grimly.

She looked at him again, gray-faced and unshaven, his eyes beginning to glow, and drew her kimono closer. 'I must go back to Mother,' she decided.

'Just a moment,' he spoke up sharply, placing his foot against the door. 'I'd like my ring back,' he said.

He held out his hand, and she glanced at him hatefully.

'You get out of my way,' she quavered.

Then, as he did not move, she stepped to the outer door, and, as she peered out, the rising sun smote her hair. It had been coiled up hastily, and the sun turned it to gold, but all he saw was a lock of hair – gone.

'My God, Penny,' he gasped, starting forward and lurching back again. 'What have you done?'

She stood in the doorway, surveying him curiously, and at the look in his eyes she flushed. Then, regardless of her will, one hand stole up her neck and covered the damning spot in her hair. She plucked it away hurriedly and turned her face, stealing a glance at him through her tumbled tresses.

'What's the matter?' she asked faintly. 'Are you sick?'

'Yes, Penny, I'm sick. I hardly know what I'm saying. Only ... I didn't think you'd do it.'

'Do what?' she demanded, flaring up at the implication. 'You're always accusing me of something!'

He again reached out his hand. 'Give me my ring ... you know what you've done.'

She twisted the ring on her finger but left it in its place. '*What* have I done?' she asked defiantly.

'I see,' he answered slowly, 'that you have lost a lock of hair. Did you give it to Keck, Penny?'

She reeled and placed one hand on the

table for support. 'He took it,' she murmured. 'Why?'

'Give me the ring!' he burst out angrily. 'My God, why discuss it? Do you pretend to love me now?'

'No,' she replied, turning deathly pale, 'but ... how did you know it, Clay?'

'I knew it when I saw that lock of hair gone. You aren't the first girl...'

'Oh!' she shrieked, and bit her lips fiercely to check the sound. 'Don't wake Mother,' she implored him. 'Now tell me.'

'Dear Penny,' he said contritely, 'I'm sorry this had to happen... I should never have gone off and left you. But now that it's done, be assured I will never tell it ... only, Penny, you must give me the ring.'

'Here it is,' she said, placing it coldly in his hand. 'I intended to give it back. But Clay, what did you mean, when you said that ... about my hair? ... about not being the first...?'

'He has done it with others, so they say.'

'Oh, they do, do they?' she repeated, her color coming back. 'You ought to be ashamed of such gossip. Jim is a gentleman and...'

'Keck's not a gentleman,' Hawks broke in ruthlessly. 'Now listen to me a minute ... this thing has gone far enough. Not only is Keck no gentleman, but he keeps these locks of hair and shows them in the saloons when he's drunk. He braids them into a scalp lock and boasts over his conquests. Is that what you call a gentleman?'

'Oh!' she screamed, clapping her hands over her ears and retreating against the wall. 'How can you be so cruel? I don't believe a word of it ... you're just saying it to wound me ... to poison my thoughts of Jim.'

'I know it,' he answered inexorably.

'*How* do you know it? Did you see it yourself? Or did you take the word of some lying enemy? There ... I can tell by your eye you've just been repeating some falsehood. I'll never forgive you, Clay.'

'Forgive me? Can you look me in the eye and explain how Keck got that lock of hair? If I were half a man, I'd...'

'He promised to marry me,' she said.

'Sure, and he promised all the rest of them. What's the word of a dog like that? My God, Penny, I can hardly believe it.'

'You don't need to be so superior,' she spat back vindictively. 'And I'm not ashamed, the least bit. What is love for anyway, if not to be given? You thought you could buy it with money. But I never did love you, and I never intended to marry you. I just used you to get out here where I'm free.'

He nodded. 'Well, you're free. What now?'

'I'm going to marry Jim Keck,' she answered resolutely. 'Oh, you don't need to smile ... I know what you're thinking but he is going to marry me. I know it.'

'What? Marry a man like that?' he burst out incredulously, and she flew at him like a fury.

'If you don't keep still I'll ... I'll *kill* you! He's a better man than you are, or ever will be. I love him, and I'm going to marry him.'

'Well, you want to hurry up, before I...'

'Before you what?' she demanded.

'Before I put him in the pen,' he said.

Chapter Ten

'What do you mean?' Penny pleaded, reading the purpose in Hawk's hard eyes. 'Oh, Clay, don't you *ever* think of my happiness?'

'He'd *kill* me, if I gave him the chance,' Hawks replied, 'so don't be foolish. I believe that's your mother coming.'

A measured step was approaching the door as Penny signaled him frantically not to tell.

'What are you children quarreling about?' inquired Mrs Pennyman from the doorway. 'Why, Clayton, I didn't know you were back.'

'I got back last night, but Keck was here before me. Penny and I have broken our engagement.'

'Oh ... again?' she cried with mock dismay. 'Well, most quarrels occur before breakfast.'

106

'I've had my breakfast,' he stated

'You look tired, Clayton,' she soothed. 'Did you have a hard ride? Oh, dear, the fire is out.'

'I'll light it,' Hawks said, 'as soon as I chop a little wood. You stayed up late last night.'

'Why, yes, we did. Were you here?'

'Outside. I saw Keck.'

'Why, Clayton, it never occurred to me that you objected to him so seriously.'

'He was your guest,' Hawks said politely, but it was the formal politeness that cloaks anger and resentment, and she went over to putter at the stove.

'And was this quarrel...,' she began, 'did you break your engagement merely because Jim Keck was our guest? Then, Penny, you must pack your trunk at once, while I am cooking breakfast. We will start for Powder Springs immediately.'

'I'll be harnessing up the horses,' Hawks said, still politely, and went off without chopping the wood.

'Oh, I think...,' Penny began as he stepped out the door, but Hawks did not linger to hear. He had been taught by his father an austere politeness toward all women, but the strain was beginning to tell, and, having committed them to the departure he kept resolutely away from them until further overture would have been abject. When he drew up to the doorway, his two saddle horses were behind the wagon, and his rifle was between his knees. There was a look in his eyes so grim and overbearing that Penny brushed away a burst of tears. Her last hope had fled, and, weeping bitterly now, she kissed her pony good bye and stepped in. Only a word from him, even so much as a kind look, and she would have begged to stay just one more day.

The presence of two pistols, in addition to Hawks's rifle, filled Mrs Pennyman with a vague alarm, but remembering his father's precepts he was the acme of politeness until he drew up before the hotel. Then, begging them to excuse him, he took his horses and the guns and rode down for an interview with William Bones. Bones was out, so he put his horses in the corral and came back to find Bones waiting.

'Well, Clay,' he smiled, 'they told me you were looking for me ... must've had a medium hard trip.'

Hawks closed the door behind him, remembering a quotation from Shakespeare that a man can smile and smile and still be a villain. 'Yes,' he said, 'and if you'd do a little more riding, you'd come nearer my idea of a manager. Every time I come into town, I find you in this office. No wonder they're stealing us blind.'

'What you need,' declared Bones, still keeping up the smile, 'is a shave and a good night's sleep. You seem to be peevish about something.'

Hawks strode over past him and closed the other door, the one that connected with the bank. 'What do you know about this Heart brand?' he asked.

'Heart brand... Heart brand?' repeated Bones irritably. 'I don't know a thing about it.'

'Well, you're one hell of a manager, that's all I'll say. You've got nerve to take the money.'

Bones sat up stiffly, glaring at Hawks under his heavy eyebrows and saw now that he was speaking in earnest. 'Any time,' he announced, 'that you don't like my way of managing things, you can have the job back ... *I* don't want it!'

'Well, you're fired, then,' rapped out Hawks. 'And Keck is fired. I'm going to wire to Rawlins for a bunch of gunmen and take over the outfit myself.'

'Gunmen?' echoed Bones, and then he laughed harshly. 'Been having some trouble with Keck. Must've cut you out with your girl.'

'You keep on getting funny,' glowered Hawks, 'and you'll find out you've picked the wrong man to monkey with. Kindly leave the lady's name strictly out of it.'

'Oh, certainly, certainly,' returned Bones with exaggerated politeness. 'Anything else I can do to accommodate you?'

'Yes, I want a complete statement of our business, up to date ... and you can turn over the cash right now.'

'Do you mean it?' demanded Bones, taken aback by Hawks's manner. 'Well, see here, now ... who am I working for ... you or your father?'

'You've been working for my father, but as soon as I touch the wire, you'll find out you're not working for anyone. Dad gave me the ranch, if I'd come out here and take charge of it, and that's just what I'm going to do. Your duties as manager have ceased.'

'What's your objection,' asked Bones, 'to the way I've been running things? Don't you think I've been faithful in my duties?'

'No, I don't, Mister Bones. The least you've been is negligent. The minute I got to town and found Keck on a drunk...'

'Aha, you're just jealous,' sneered Bones.

'Did you ever hear of the Heart brand?' inquired Hawks.

'What's biting you?' countered Bones after glaring at him a minute. 'You seem to have something on your mind.'

'I have,' stated Hawks, 'something important. Mister Bones, under your management, we lost eight hundred head of steers, worth at least twenty dollars apiece ... that comes to sixteen thousand, right there. And besides that I found calves, sucking Lazy B cows, with a big Heart burned on their hip. You never heard of the Heart brand, you say.'

'Well, I've heard of it,' acknowledged Bone, 'seen a few on the range, but I never did know who owned it.'

'And you think your wagon boss, Jim Keck, is capable and honest, even if he does come to town and get drunk?'

'I'll swear to it,' Bones asserted stoutly.

'I'll report this to Dad,' nodded Hawks.

'Now, here,' challenged Bones, bringing his chair down with a thump, 'you tell me what you know, straight out. I don't allow no man to make insinuations against my character... I'm honest, even if I do make mistakes. What's all this talk leading up to?'

For an answer Hawks leaned over and, taking a slip of paper, drew a Lazy B brand, while Bones stared. Then with a couple of flips he extended the wings, forming a Heart below the bar. 'Our brand is being burned,' he said.

'Yes, but gosh A'mighty, man, look at that bar going across there.'

'That's been hair-branded, right under your nose.'

'W'y, what son-of-a-bitch...?' marveled Bones.

'Your own wagon boss ... Keck ... and his gang.'

'I don't believe it!' Bones shouted defiantly.

'You don't have to,' returned Hawks. 'I've

got this evidence to prove it. Is the sheriff in this county any good?'

'Now, here,' argued Bones, twisting his head to one side and showing his teeth belligerently, 'what's the use of showing me up? I've been negligent, and I admit it, but the best of us make mistakes. I don't want this taken out of my hands.'

'You've been worse than negligent,' answered Hawks indignantly. 'You've opposed me from the start and stood in with Keck. You've stood by him, right or wrong, and the best I could get out of you was some low, coarse crack about Penny. You've done me an injury that you can never repay.'

Hawks looked at him so sternly that Bones squirmed in his seat, for he felt the unspoken tragedy behind his words. 'I'm sorry,' he apologized lamely. 'Never thought it wasn't all right. Anything I can do, Clay, don't fail to let me know.'

'The first thing you can do,' spoke up Hawks, 'is to send out a caretaker to look after that ranch house before those Texans burn it down. Let me tell you what kind of an outfit we're up against.'

He ran over circumstantially all that Rooster Raslem had told him, carefully concealing the source of his knowledge, and, when he had ended, Bones leaned back in his chair and called down heartfelt curses on Keck. Then he sat a long time silently, matching the tips of his fingers together while is ferret eyes were glazed in thought. He did not look honest, even then, but Hawks was satisfied his intentions were good. Either that or he was a play actor, instead of a money-lender who imagined himself a cowman. That was the trouble with William Bones. He was still a thrifty farmer, pinching pennies where he should be riding horses down. He had trusted his wagon boss too far.

'Clay,' he said at last, 'I got you into this jackpot, and I'm going to get you out. Them steers ain't all gone, only that two hundred head that they crossed on the ice last winter. The rest are out in the cedars. Now you turn this over to me, and I'll guarantee to get them steers back ... that's better than shooting it out with Keck. Yes, I know how you feel, but I'm responsible to your father... I lost them steers and I'll return 'em, whatever's left ... but, if you ride in on that gang with a bunch of gunmen from Rawlins, they'll start something, and you'll lose the whole herd. Them cattle are in Colorado, and Wyoming warrants are no use anyway ... what we want is to get the steers ... and the only way to do it is to keep dark ... understand? ... until we can find out where they air. Now here's my proposition, and you can take it or leave it. I submit it for what it's worth. We go down to my ranch, which is in Bear County, Colorado, and get all my cowpunchers deputized, then we ride back to the Lazy B and tell Keck I've bought the outfit and we're going to have a range count, right now. If there's anything crooked, that's the sure way to find out, but what them fellows will do is to high-tail it for the Vermilion and start to drive off them steers. Then all we've got to do is to follow after 'em with our deputies, and they can't possibly get away. And while we're about it, we'll clean up on Telford Payne.'

There was the devil's hoof again – Bones never forgot his grudge against Payne – but his plan seemed a good one, and less than a week later Hawks rode up to Keck's wagon with a posse. Bones was there beside him, a cumbersome rifle on his saddle and his old .45 in his belt, and behind them rode eleven men with pistols and saddle guns in evidence. It was along toward noon, but all the Texans were at the wagon. Each man wore two six-shooters and from the glint in Keck's eyes it was evident that he was fore-warned. He knew what they had in mind.

'Mister Keck,' began Bones with a wolfish grin, 'we've come over here to have a roundup and range count. This here ranch is losing money, and, as Hawks is dissatisfied, I've taken the Lazy B off his hands.'

'Very well, seh,' bowed Keck, favoring Hawks with a mocking smile. 'I have no objections, I'm sure.'

'We'll count the mesa here first,' went on Bones importantly, 'and then the lower range. If any of you boys would like to keep on, you can help till the roundup is done.'

There was a long minute of silence as the Texans exchanged glances, and the posse opened out expectantly.

'How about me?' whined Uncle Simmy, limping up to the front with a six-shooter low at his hip. 'Do I hold my job, or go?'

'You go,' announced Bones. 'Your cooking is too wasteful. From now on things are going to be different.'

'Yes ... sowbelly and beans,' spoke up a big Texan disdainfully. 'You can give me my time, right now.'

'I'll take mine, too,' jeered another, and, as Bones whipped out his checkbook, they all called for their time, except Keck. He lounged easily by a wagon wheel where their saddle guns were stacked, looking on with an impish grin.

'I done blowed my time,' he laughed, 'for six months in advance, so there's no use mentioning payment. Come on, boys, I'm burned out on the Lazy B.'

He stepped up on his private mount, which was saddled and waiting, and picked up the rope of his pack horse.

'Good day, gentlemen,' he bowed. 'I hope you find all satisfactory. We shore worked hard, didn't we, boys?'

There was a rumble of sarcastic laughter from the band of Texans, and then they rode off, heading south.

Chapter Eleven

The first skirmish had been a draw, except that in the excitement several Texans had ridden off on Lazy B horses. It was a bold thing to do, but if anybody took notice, it was allowed to pass at the time. They were a hard-working outfit, evidently fully prepared for trouble, and any controversy might have brought on shooting, so, with his eye on the main chance, Bones pocketed the insult and spread a new net for their feet. But first he packed off Uncle Simmy, who was waspish as a rattlesnake, lest his plans should be revealed a second time.

His first carefully laid plot had been betrayed to the enemy, and, without naming any names, he gave Hawks to understand that he suspected a certain young lady. She had been seen in Jim Keck's company the day after Hawks left town, and God only knew what had happened since – she was certainly crazy over that cowboy. Bones added naïvely that if he'd known then what he knew later, he'd have been a little more careful what he said to her. Hawks let this subject drop, for in an ill-advised moment he had spoken a word too much to Penny himself. He had told her, if she was going to marry Keck, she would have to hurry up before he put him in the pen.

At sight of the wagon boss, lolling so nonchalantly among his henchmen, Hawks had felt a surging impulse to shoot him. Not only had Keck robbed him of a small fortune in cattle, but he had seduced his fiancée. Yes, he had been able to claim a love lock from Penny's foolish head while Hawks's ring still gleamed on her finger, and something told Hawks now that, over and beyond Keck's love of sexual conquest, was a desire to strike a blow at an enemy. He had devised a hellish insult – he had stepped between Hawks and his promised bride. Then, as Keck had glanced up at him, Hawks read his secret laughter, the leering insolence of the man. But Hawks had turned this raid over to that arch blunderer, William Bones, and given his word not to shoot. Bones's plan had been a good one, but Hawks already repented his bargain for, face to face with the bold Texans, Bones had been euchred at every turn. He had given men their time checks and then stood by gawking while they rode off on Lazy B mounts. What a laugh they must be having among themselves!

Yet if Bones's plan was to work at all, in

order to lull the suspicion of the Texans they began the first circle of their roundup. That gather was enough to prove beyond a doubt that the Lazy B calves were being hair branded. Working on Hawks's own time, and within sight of his ranch house, they had been preparing to steal still more calves. Only the mother cows carried a straight Lazy B brand. It was a humiliating day for Bones, in the presence of his own cowboys, to have his gullibility thus shown up, and, as soon as it was dark, he sent two of his riders to spy on Keck's gang. If his crafty scheme succeeded and they won back the stolen steers, these mistakes would be like sacrificing pawns to capture kings.

The wagon was started south the next day to be that much nearer to the battle ground, but hardly were they moving when one of their scouts topped the rim and beckoned them frantically with his hat. He rode his horse in short circles, the Indian sign for game and haste, and the posse broke into a lope. Leading the chase to the rim, Hawks saw at a glance that the rustlers had stolen a march. The dust of their moving herd showed far down Vermilion Wash, and, as they spurred to intercept them, the plume of their dust cloud disappeared down the vent of Vermilion Cañon. The rustlers had won again, carrying on their roundup by moonlight and making their escape into Coon

Hole. Hawks was for following pell-mell after them, but, fearing an ambush, Bones led the posse east through the cedars. When they gazed down into the Hole, the cattle were nearly across it, and the sun was setting red through their dust.

That night they brought up the horse cavvy and, with fresh mounts and packs of provisions, pressed on across the basin at dawn. But the hardihood of the rustlers led to the hidden Robbers' Trail. Where a ledge of lime made a clear space among the cedars, the posse came to a high, level bench and, following up an open draw, Hawks caught sight of a few stragglers disappearing through the portals of a pass. On both sides, like a ribbed wall, the rim rose before them, its summit crowned with pines and firs, and the gateway through which the herd had passed was no wider than the cast of a rope. Three panels of fence and an unbarred gate showed that cattle had been held there before, but not a man in the posse had ever penetrated into the no man's land that lay beyond the rim. All they knew was that the trail led into a huge pocket of a basin, cut off on the west by the abysmal Cañon of the Green River and on the south by the Cañon of the Bear.

'We've got 'em!' announced Bones, after they had talked the matter over, and led off at the head of the posse. There were others more competent both to lead and to track, but a devilish impatience seemed to have laid hold upon William Bones, and he spurred his horse to the front. He rode like an Indian, kicking his heels at every step, muttering threats at the rustlers they had trapped, but as he rounded a point, a bullet struck in front of him, and in the scramble he was nearly unhorsed. As that bullet whined over his head, there was a smash against a pine tree and another against a rock, and, after they had all taken cover, they saw the smoke of black powder rifles, jetting out from the portals of the pass. The rustlers had made a stand.

'By cracky, boys, this is dangerous!' exclaimed Bones to his cowboys. 'We can never get through that pass ... one man could hold back a thousand. What say we go back to Coon Hole?'

'Coon Hole!' echoed Hawks. 'What do you want to go there for? The steers are over this rim.'

'Yes, and about forty rustlers, all shooting to kill. Uhn-huh, Mister Hawks, it's too dangerous.'

Hawks looked around at the grim faces of the cowboys and caught the eye of the under-sheriff – the one who had come along to do the deputizing. 'Who'll go with me up that rim on foot?' he asked, and they all spoke up at once.

'I got no business in Coon Hole,' said the under-sheriff significantly, and Bones found himself on the defensive.

'Well, now, here, boys,' he hedged, 'mebbe I was a little too precipitate ... I never thought of climbing up them ledges ... but here's the way it looks to me. Tel Payne and his gang ... and all them Coon Hole cedar-snappers ... are bottled up as tight as a drumhead ... they've come over here to help drive these cattle. Now! Ain't this the chance of a lifetime to cut old Tel's herd, leaving him nothing except what carries his straight brand? He's been stealing off of all of us, and he's got burned stuff from everywhere, but nothing with a barred brand goes. Make him show a bill of sale or seize every vented cow he's got ... we can come back and get these steers later.'

'Yes, but maybe they won't be here,' Hawks objected angrily. 'Maybe they'll drive 'em across the river into Utah. We've been fiddling and fooling around until I've got a bellyful, myself. Come on, Howard, you're the boss. Let's go after 'em.'

'Suits me,' returned the under-sheriff with a baleful glare at Bones. 'It's been said,' he went on, 'that the sheriff and his deputies are afraid to do their duties in Bear County. I want to make it plain, right now, that here's one under-sheriff that ain't afraid to go anywhere!'

'Well, all right, boys,' capitulated Bones, 'this is an awful risky business...'

'Risky, hell!' snorted the under-sheriff. 'This is my regular line of duty. Come on, boys ... take your spurs off ... let's start.'

It was a long and dangerous climb up the shelving heights of the rimrock, but they gained the summit about noon, only to find the portals below them deserted. The rustlers had sensed an attack from above and retreated up the cañon after the herd. From the pine-clad heights the six men who had made the ascent could look down into the no man's land beyond, and, far out across the waste of sagebrush and cedared hills, they could see the dust of the herd. It was still moving south, and, darting about in the rear, they could make out the harrying horsemen, but what they saw was only the tail of the long, snake-like trail herd, disappearing through a gap in the hills. Where the high ridge to the east pushed out across the basin, a jagged peak thrust up among low hills, and west of that ran the wooded lip of the great cañon, making the gorge of the Green River far below. All beyond seemed still more forbidding, if not impassable, and, whichever way it went, the trail would end at the brink of a chasm, for Bear River was only a short distance south. There seemed no escape, yet the outlaws were still fleeing, and Howard signaled for the horses to be brought up.

Minutes dragged by like hours, and one hour dragged into two before Bones and the rear posse came up, and, as they dashed across the mesa on the trail of the rustlers, even Bones forgot his fears. At last they were in the open, and, on the wings of the wind, they could hear the distant bellowing of the herd.

'What's that?' exclaimed the under-sheriff as they halted on a rise to look out over the country ahead. 'It's shooting ... can't you hear that big gun?'

They strained their ears to listen, and, above the distant lowing, they could hear a faint popping, like the sputtering of wet coals in a fire.

'There!' cried the under-sheriff. 'Didn't you hear that Forty-Five-Ninety? There's been shooting down there for some time.'

'Must be fighting among themselves,' suggested an excited cowboy. 'Either that or another posse is after 'em.'

'Something funny's going on,' observed the under-sheriff to Hawks. 'Sounds like down by the river to me.'

'They're crossing 'em into Utah, I'll bet you,' returned Hawks. 'Come on, or we'll lose the whole herd.'

He started forward at a lope, and once more they rounded a point and ran into a spatter of bullets. But no horses went down, and, racing down into the next swale, they called a hasty council of war. The firing this time was from the slopes of a wooded hill, behind which the herd had vanished, and, while Bones, as before, stayed behind with the pack animals, Hawks and the under-sheriff's picked cowboys rode west. The country drained off here toward the invisible side cañon down which the steers had been driven, and by circling the hill they hoped to cut the trailing herd and engage the rustlers in battle. Following the cutbank of a wash, they presently entered a deeper one that led south around the hill into a third, but their movements had been noted, and, as they approached the main cañon, they were met by the rapid fire of Winchesters.

'Cut around 'em, boys!' yelled Howard. 'We'll ride clean to the river ... they can't head us off from that!'

They turned back and tried again, but the rim of the Grand Cañon seemed swarming with hostile riflemen. The distant firing had almost ceased, the bellowing of cattle was only an echo of what had been long in their ears, and now the bullets came so fast that, although no one was hit, they decided to return to their packs. If it ever came to war, they were clearly outnumbered, although the rustlers did not shoot to kill. They seemed fully satisfied to stand off the posse while the herd was being crossed below. But was it being crossed? Hawks for one could not believe it, for he had seen the sweep of the Green River above. Where it flowed into its cañon neither man nor horse could swim it, and here its rush would be tremendous. Yet Keck had accomplished the impossible so often that Hawks feared he might still lose his herd.

'Hey! Don't shoot, boys!' hailed Bones as they rode up the wash. 'There's a party going to get them to surrender!'

'What party?' yelled Hawks, enraged at the delay. 'What do you expect us to do ... sit down and wait?'

'That was the agreement,' smirked Bones. 'There was a lady came by here, claiming to be Keck's wife ... she had rode down with Uncle Simmy, the cook ... and she said, if we'd stop shooting and let her see her husband, she knew she could get him to surrender.'

'Yes, but what about those steers?' shouted Hawks without listening to him. 'Maybe they're running them off into the brush. I didn't make any such agreement, and I'm not going to be bound by it. Come on, Howard, let's try a circle east.'

'I'll go you,' answered Howard. 'If they shoot, by grab, we'll shoot back.'

They rode off through the sagebrush, still followed by the four cowboys, and, since nobody fired at them as they came into the main trail, the under-sheriff-spurred down it at a gallop. Hawks and the cowboys rode after him, openly defying the hidden outlaws who allowed them to pass unscathed. Around the wooded hill they swung west down the dusty path where the great herd had trailed off down the cañon. Over rocks and through quaking asps they pounded on down the steep slope until they pulled up on the brink of a surging mass of cattle on a sandbar. Behind them in a phalanx stretched a solid line of cowboys, and, as they listened, they heard muffled reports.

'They're shooting them!' yelped the under-sheriff. 'They're trying to destroy the evidence. Come on, boys ... all we need is just one!'

Once more they fought their way down the trail the cattle had traveled, a trail that seemed impassable, but, when they got to the bottom and rode out on the sandbar, the rest of Hawks's steers was gone. Twenty men came trotting toward them, with Keck at their head, and by his side rode Penny, smiling.

Chapter Twelve

Surprise and anger held Hawks speechless as he confronted a cattle thief and found Charlotte Pennyman beside him.

Howard, the under-sheriff, found his tongue. 'Stop right there,' he ordered, holding one hand against them while the other reached for his gun. 'You're under arrest ... the whole outfit.'

'For what?' inquired Keck, reining in his wet horse defiantly, and the rustlers wheeled in behind him.

'For stealing cattle,' returned the under-sheriff grimly.

'Hain't stole no cattle,' challenged Keck. 'Show me any cow that I stole.'

The under-sheriff frowned and glanced dubiously at Hawks. 'Will you swear out a warrant?' he asked.

'Just a moment, seh!' protested Keck, pointing a gloved finger at the under-sheriff. 'I happen to know the law.'

'You don't observe it,' flared back the under-sheriff. 'I saw you myself ... driving those cattle into the river and drowning them.'

'Where's your evidence to prove it?'

sneered Keck. 'A man is presumed to be innocent till he's proven guilty.'

'I saw a stray ... back there,' spoke up a cowboy deputy.

The under-sheriff drew his gun. 'Go back and find it,' he ordered, without turning his head, 'and don't let no man take it away from you. I'll ask all you gentlemen to remain right here.'

He balanced his six-shooter, ready at the first move to throw down and shoot, but it was six against twenty, and the rustlers were not the men to submit meekly to arrest. There were too many with rewards on their heads. They began to mill among themselves, grumbling and protesting louder and louder, and, as the spirit of revolt emboldened the more daring, they began to scatter out and drift off.

'Come back here!' barked the under-sheriff as Curly Bill, the Negro cowboy, started his horse off up the ravine.

'What for, suh?' he complained. 'Ah ain't stole no cattle.'

'You stole that horse!' charged Hawks, reining out to turn him back. 'It's got my brand on its hip. Go back there, damn your heart, or I'll kill you.'

'Now, heah!' spoke up Keck.

As Hawks whirled on Keck, eyes aflame, Penny rode in between them and faced Hawks.

'We're married now,' she said. 'Please don't quarrel with my husband, Clay. And they surrender ... don't you, boys? You know you promised.'

'I'll surrender,' assented Keck, turning to address the under-sheriff, 'but not to him ... understand?' He jerked a scornful thumb in the direction of Hawks.

The under-sheriff nodded briefly. 'You're my prisoner,' he said, 'and I want Curly Bill, too. The rest of your gentlemen are excused. But stay behind,' he ordered as they started to romp ahead. 'And leave that stray strictly alone!'

They fell in behind, some grumbling, some voicing openly disrespect for the law, but the under-sheriff allowed their remarks to pass unnoticed, for he found himself in a tight. Instead of Keck and his six cowboys, he found himself confronted by over twenty desperate outlaws, some of whom he knew by their photographs, and besides that he suddenly realized that he was in the heart of rustler country, where no officer's life was safe. Hence his magnanimous action in dismissing all the cattle thieves with the exception of Jim Keck and Curly Bill. He would be lucky to get away with those two – but for Penny he would have let them all go.

'Must have been a hard ride, ma'am,' he said as he led off up the cañon with Penny close behind him. 'Much obliged for helping me out with these men.'

'Oh, don't mention it,' she smiled. 'I'm Missus Keck, you know ... we've only been married a week.'

'You don't say!' exclaimed the under-sheriff, turning to eye her curiously, but he left his thoughts unsaid.

'Yes, and, when I received word that this trouble had come up, I rode clear from Powder Springs with the cook.'

The under-sheriff's eyes shifted to the sinister visage of Uncle Simmy, and once more what he thought remained unsaid.

'I knew my husband wasn't guilty,' she went on impulsively, 'so I rode down to get him to surrender. He's from Texas, you know, and...'

'Yes, I savvy,' nodded the under-sheriff. 'Here comes the rest of them.'

They had ascended to the first bench where, in a thicket of quaking aspens, Bones and his posse were trying to flog out the sullen stray.

'Well, well!' exclaimed Bones as Penny gave him a tired smile. 'Wasn't looking to see you down here. So you're Missus Keck now?'

'Yes,' she beamed. 'Sorry you couldn't be present. We were married the day after you left.'

'Too late to kiss the bride,' he observed, with a smirk at Hawks. 'Have you congratulated 'em yet, Clay?'

'No,' Hawks answered absently, still keeping his eyes on the stray that was being dragged out on a rope. 'Is that one of those Utah steers?'

'W'y, yes,' assented Bones, after a look at the brand. 'Where's all the rest of them, Clay?'

'In the river,' he replied. 'On their way down the Grand Cañon. This is all we've got left, Mister Bones.'

'Well, well!' exclaimed Bones again. 'The whole six hundred head?'

'As many as there were, they're gone.'

Bones screwed up his mouth and gazed about at the bedraggled rustlers who were looking him over sourly. 'What about them?' he asked. 'Have you placed them under arrest?'

'Only Keck and Curly Bill,' answered the under-sheriff curtly. 'We can't prove the ownership of those steers.'

'Well, what about this one?' demanded Bones. 'Is this your steer, Mister Keck?'

'No, seh,' smiled Keck, 'it is not.'

'Ain't that your brand?' broke in the under-sheriff, pointing accusingly at the Heart that was burned in the stray steer's hip.

'My brand, seh, yes, but not my steer. Some enemy of mine has put it on this critter in order to get me involved with the law.'

'You damned cow thief,' broke in the under-sheriff, pointing accusingly at the Heart burned on the stray steer's hip. 'Now, here,' he said, laying a restraining hand on Hawks, 'don't pick no fight with my prisoner. He's surrendered to the law, and he's under my protection until I deliver him into the custody of the sheriff.'

'Well, keep him away from me, then,' returned Hawks, his eyes blazing, 'or I won't be responsible for what happens. I'll stay behind and look after this steer.'

'Good enough,' agreed the under-sheriff. 'I'll leave six men to help you.' And he departed with his prisoners up the cañon.

It was a long trip to Cody, a half deserted mining town over on Bear River, and a longer wait for the trial, and the moment that Penny took her place on the witness stand Hawks knew he had lost his case. She testified, among other things, to having been engaged to Mr. Hawks, in whose employ Mr. Keck had been, and that, when she had informed Hawks she was going to marry Keck, he had made a definite threat against her husband. He had told her she had better hurry up before he put Keck in the pen. Yes, she understood the pen to mean the penitentiary. Mr. Hawks had appeared to be clearly jealous of his wagon boss.

It was a bitter pill to swallow, and, when Keck was acquitted, Hawks told them to turn Curly Bill loose, before Penny appeared for *him*. Then he washed his hands of her and of the whole proceedings and, incidentally, of Bear County law. His range was in Wyoming, most of the jury had been rustler sympathizers, and Bones had done his share to wreck their case. He was not very popular in Bear County, especially with the officers of the law, and a high-priced Denver lawyer, engaged by Penny to defend her husband, had tied up Hawks in a knot. The whole trial had been a farce, the six hundred steers were a total loss, and the best thing for Hawks to do was to go back to his ranch and try to protect what was left.

The new cowpunchers that he engaged were not exactly gunmen, but at the same time they were hired for their nerve, and to obviate the possibility of having any more like Keck in his employ he took the job of wagon boss himself. Then, having raked the lower range and re-branded his hair-branded calves, he bethought himself of the residue in Coon Hole. At the trial, Keck had admitted that he owned the Heart brand, but he claimed that Hawks's calves had been burned without his knowledge by enemies who sought to incriminate him. All that had the straight Heart brand he had acknowledged as his property, but he had disclaimed all those whose brands had been burned over. Therefore, according to his own statement, the mavericked calves in Coon Hole still belonged to the Lazy B.

Perhaps it was a rankling sense of the injuries he had suffered that made Hawks's thoughts turn toward Coon Hole, even a willingness to pick a fight with the cattle thief, for, promptly after his wife had secured Keck's release on bail, Keck had returned to Coon Hole. At the lower end of the valley – where Green River, flowing into its cañon, gave a wonderful view from their front door – he and Penny had built a home out of logs, fitting it up with every luxury to be imagined. The story had traveled far about the Brussels carpet on their floor, the model kitchen, and the grand piano; and one room was nearly filled with the wedding gifts Penny had received, including cut glass and solid silver with her monogram. All this was in a log house that soon became the rendezvous of all the rustlers associated with Keck and his gang – the same ruthless men who, unable to cross them into Utah, had destroyed six hundred head of Hawks's steers.

The thought of those big steers, fat and ready for market, floating off down Green River in windrows always left Clayton Hawks seeing red, and, when he rode back into Coon Hole with his cowboys behind him, there was still a baleful glint in his eye.

He was not hunting for trouble, but, law or no law, he was out to get his full legal rights. They rode up to the Payne ranch half an hour after sunrise, having entered the Hole at night, and, when Telford Payne came out and saw the men behind Hawks, he was almost civil in his greeting.

'Good morning, Mister Payne,' returned Hawks politely. 'Just down looking for some Lazy B strays. Any objections to my cutting that herd?' He jerked his head toward the cattle grazing below them.

Payne glanced up at the ridge. 'None whatever,' he said.

'I might explain,' went on Hawks, 'that the cattle I'm looking for are some that Keck stole. He altered my brand to a Heart, but at the trial he stated specifically that he laid no claim to any burned stuff. Anything, he said, that was not in his straight brand had been burned over by his enemies. Do you claim any interest in those Heart calves?'

'None whatever,' stated Payne decidedly.

'Good enough,' pronounced Hawks. 'I hope it won't cause any inconvenience if my cowboys ride through your pasture?'

'No, sir,' replied Payne. 'It will not.'

'Very kind of you,' murmured Hawks, and he was reining away when Mrs Payne stepped out the door. Even at this early hour her hair was smoothly brushed, her house dress was immaculately clean, and, as she hurried down the walk, passing her husband as he went in, Hawks could not but notice the difference in their step. His was that of an old man, firm and resolute but slow, while she walked as lightly as a deer.

'Good morning!' she called, and, as Hawks returned the greeting, his cowboys all took off their hats. 'Good morning, boys,' she said, meeting their admiring glances frankly. 'Have you had your breakfast yet?'

'Yes, ma'am,' they responded, and, after looking at each one of them, she turned her eyes upon Hawks.

'Going down to make your call on the bride?' she bantered.

'Why, no, Missus Payne,' he replied unsmilingly. 'This is purely a business trip. All right, boys,' he said to the men, 'we'll round up the pasture first, and be careful not to chouse them around.'

He was starting off again, having no stomach for woman's gossip, when Mrs Payne beckoned him back urgently. 'You'd better look out,' she warned. 'They're watching you from the ridge.'

'All right,' he said. 'Much obliged.'

'And if you'll take my advice,' she added, 'you'll whip out of Coon Hole right soon.'

'We just got in,' he answered with a grin, and rode off to look at the herd.

There was nothing in Payne's pasture that he could lay any claim to, so, remembering her warning, he spread his men across the flat and rode rapidly back toward the east. For some reason or other the Heart cattle he had seen before had disappeared from the meadows along the Vermilion, but as they worked back toward Irish Cañon, they began to pick up strays that had been altered from Lazy B to Heart. Their ears were still unhealed where the swallow-fork in the left had been cut down to a grub, and it came over Hawks that he was still losing calves, that even yet they were working his range. In spite of his line riders they were picking up hair-burned calves and pushing them over the divide into Coon Hole.

But gathering these strays had taken time, and, as he pressed on up the trail, Hawks was brought to a realization of what Rooster Raslem had told him. From the mouth of Irish Cañon two horsemen rode out and ducked back into their ambush, a peak out on the flat gave up its man, and, as they moved on toward Vermilion Cañon, a flying streak of dust told of riders in hot pursuit. They were caught in the open, and, seeing the leaders riding around him, Hawks bunched up his cattle and waited. One man on the ground is the equal of two or three mounted, but the rustlers were not seeking a fight. Having brought them to a stand, the outlaws rode in slowly, their right hands held up for peace, and Hawks beckoned the foremost to approach. They all moved in at that, and, as he scanned their hard faces, Hawks recognized several of the old gang that had driven his steers into Green River – and Keck was there with the rest. Keck advanced a trifle dubiously, with Curly Bill and his Texans around him, and, when Hawks held up his hand, they stopped.

'What's all this?' inquired Keck after a moment's silent scrutiny. 'Driving off a bunch of my calves?'

'They're my calves,' stated Hawks, 'burned over the Lazy B., You must think you can pick me like a Christmas tree.'

'Oh, no, Mister Hawks,' replied Keck good-naturedly, 'but there seems to be a slight difference of opinion. I claim everything in Colorado in the Heart brand.'

'When you were tried,' accused Hawks, 'you testified under oath that you claimed nothing but the straight Heart brand.'

'What I said in court is one thing, outside is another... I came to get those calves, Mister Hawks.'

'Well, come and get 'em,' invited Hawks. 'You can try to run over me, but you'd better come a-shooting.'

'I'll get 'em,' promised Keck, 'but there won't be no shooting ... that is ... not started by me.'

'I'll start it,' promised Hawks, 'if you crowd in any closer. I've taken enough from

138

you, Keck.'

'Well, I see the little lady is coming up over yonder ... we'll leave it to her to decide.'

Hawks settled back grimly, his mind firmly made up that Penny would settle nothing for him. It was humiliating enough to remember that he once had loved her and that she had inveigled him into taking her West without having it forced upon him that she had since married this cowboy and now had set up to be queen of the rustlers. These cattle were his, and he would keep them.

Penny rode up at a gallop with a few belated stragglers in her wake and came fearlessly into the midst of them. Seeing her husband, she trotted her horse over to join him while the rustlers gathered about them. Hawks shifted his gun and looked on expectantly, and presently Penny rode toward him. Her eyes were bright with excitement, the wind had had its way with her hair, and she smiled as she used to do to beguile him.

'No,' Hawks said shortly, 'you'll arbitrate nothing. And if you value that cattle thief you've got for a husband, you'll advise him that these calves are mine.'

'But *are* they yours?' she questioned

Meeting her innocent eyes, his lips curled up in a smile. 'Did your husband,' he asked, 'ever buy a single cow? Has he bought one since he came to this country? These calves are mine, and I'll keep them.'

139

She glanced back at Jim Keck and the rough men gathered about him, and the glad light went out of her eyes. 'Won't you show me the brands?' she asked, 'so I can go back and report what they are? And please don't be hateful, Clay.'

'Go and look at 'em,' he said. 'I don't give a damn whether these rustlers think they own 'em or not.'

Penny rode over to the band of seared and ear-marked yearlings, scanning their brands with vacant eyes, then without another word she turned back to the waiting rustlers, shaking her head as they all questioned her at once.

'My mistake,' called Jim Keck, waving a carefully gloved hand at Hawks, and rode off with Penny and all of his men.

Chapter Thirteen

Hawks and his cowboys smiled grimly among themselves at the phrase Keck had employed. *My mistake* was good enough as an euphemistic expression, conveying the idea that he yielded the point, but the king of the rustlers had been bluffed out of his boots and compelled to beat a retreat. In the presence of Penny and all his thieving followers he had backed down and let Hawks keep his calves – he had allowed nine men to ride into Coon Hole and defy him to cut their herd. Hawks drove the calves safely home, but when he started his fall roundup, he found that the rustlers had taken their revenge. In spite of his line riders the lower range had been combed clean and several hundred more calves had disappeared.

Here in a way was Keck's answer to the defiance that had been hurled into his teeth, but in another way it was only the working out of a law as old as nature itself. When a pair of wolves invade the range, they kill for themselves alone, but when their cubs are grown up, they run in packs and kill for the pleasure of the chase. The cedar-snappers of Coon Hole, like a neglected den of wolves, had increased until they ran in packs, and now, riding at night, they stole Lazy B calves and would continue until they were driven off or killed. The times had changed since Sam Hawks had ridden this range, a law unto himself. The day was past when a man could arm his cowboys and ride in and hang presumptuous rustlers, and yet the day had not come when the officers of the law could give protection to honest cattlemen.

Hawks thought it all over as the roundup went on, revealing more losses each day, and then, bending to the storm, he ordered the whole lower range cleared – for it was either that or fight. All the badmen in the West were filtering into Coon Hole, and every man was a wolf. There were two packs now – the 'Dobe Town gang of train robbers and the rustlers that made their headquarters with Jim Keck – but all of them were eating his beef. They had to eat – Hawks knew it – but he did not have to feed them, and he retreated with his herds to Hawks Mesa. There, with line camps along the rim, he stood guard over his cows, and the wolf-pack took warning and passed him by.

All winter there were rumors of strange cowboys riding the range and of stray steers drifting in bands before the storms, but when the spring roundup came, all the strays had disappeared and tremendous losses of steers were reported. Utah brands were found in Wyoming and Wyoming brands in Utah. The Snake River winter ranges had been stripped, and, as the cattlemen compared notes, it soon became evident that organized rustlers were at work. Northern cattle had been driven south and crossed into Utah, and southern cattle driven north into Wyoming. At a call from William Bones, the principal stock raisers of the district met at his office for a private conference.

If Bones had questioned Hawks's judgment when he had abandoned his lower range and wintered his cows on the bleak mesa, the spring roundup brought its own answer. Where others had lost their hundreds, Bones, by actual count, was short nearly a thousand head. Most of his steers had been driven off during a heavy storm, and even his cows and calves had been preyed upon. Every trail that left his range had ended, sooner or later, in Coon Hole. And the new sheriff of Bear County, after sundry excuses, had finally admitted he had not captured any rustlers.

It had gotten beyond the law, or so Bones said, and, while others were less outspoken, it was agreed that something should be done. Hawks refused to commit himself, for he saw in Bones's eye a desire to push him into the forefront of the battle. Bones was for cleaning out Coon Hole, but not with his own hands – he thought Hawks would make a better leader. He was perfectly willing to do the organizing and collecting, but the leadership should go to Hawks. Just the name would make men think of old Sam Hawks, and, when Sam put on his war paint, there was a scattering. He would have cleaned out Coon Hole in one day.

Hawks listened and smiled indulgently, for some of these lost steers that Bones was raving about had been put in on Hawks's lower range. With apologies, to be sure, and veiled references to Hawks's father and what he would think to see his winter range abandoned, Bones had put in a bunch of steers, and his own cowboys had joined the rustlers, driving the whole herd off into Coon Hole. That was the way Bones preferred to tell it, but it was rumored around the saloons that the process had been reversed. Bones had hired some rustlers, thinking he was getting honest 'punchers and they had never stopped till they struck the Hole. But whether they were rustlers or honest 'punchers, they had not been so mean as to carry off their winter supplies. The sow-belly and beans had been ditched at Irish Lake to express their derision and scorn.

Hawks had not quarreled with Bones, but when he put the steers in on his range, he recalled what Mrs. Payne had said. According to her, Bones's sole reason for making war on them was to get possession of Coon Hole for a winter range. Had he planned to get Hawks's range, instead? That was a question, of course, that was now purely academic, since the cedar-snappers had stolen all the steers, but, after all, Hawks had suffered from Bones's bungling and mismanagement, and he did not feel called upon to be Bones's catspaw in Coon Hole. If Bones wanted it for his winter range, let him go down and take it, the way Sam Hawks would have done. And besides, Hawks was not losing stock. He had hired trustworthy men to ride the rim of his high stronghold, and he did a little riding himself, hence Hawks, of all the cattlemen, had had the least cause to worry about the depredations of Jim Keck's gang.

There were conferences and heated arguments, and Bones's plans were coming to nothing when a spark set off the meeting. A train came backing in, the whistle hooting raucously, and, as they crowded about the station, the word was passed along.

'Another hold-up! Train robbed ... up at Clifton!'

It had been Sundance Thorp again – Sundance and the 'Dobe Town gang – and they had headed in the direction of Coon Hole. Just the name was enough, and, when the railroad detectives arrived, they found a posse of twenty cattlemen waiting. Bones was there, and Hawks, and all the Snake River cowmen, and along with the local officers and a carload of detectives they swept out of town at a gallop. But it was a race for the rewards more than a pursuit of vicious criminals, and, as they cut a fresh trail leading down Irish Cañon, the detectives jumped into the lead. They had brought their own horses in the special stock car that the railroad had fitted up for that purpose, and the thought of twenty thousand dollars on Sundance alone made them forget the desperate chances they took.

But Sundance and his gang had not stopped to lie in ambush. They were heading for the cedar brakes of Coon Hole, and, when the rest of the posse came stringing out of Irish Cañon, the chase was far to the west. The Payne house was deserted when they finally rode up to it, and the detectives were still spurring west, but since Sundance and his three partners had changed horses at the ranch, any further pursuit seemed useless. After riding half the night and a good part of the day, the posse was ready to quit, and, when Mrs Payne appeared and offered to make them some coffee, they let the reward-hunters go. But hardly had they unsaddled their trembling mounts when there was a rattle of shots from below. Back went the sweaty saddles, and once more the race was on, down the trail toward Green River Cañon. It was a long and weary chase, the horses half dead with fatigue, but, as they rode up over the point and looked off down the river, they could see dismounted men climbing up over the huge terraces of broken sandstone.

Puffs of smoke from among the cedar showed where a running fight was in progress along the very brink of the chasm, but for the most part all was still, and only sulking forms showed where the manhunters closed in on their prey. Sundance Thorp and his men had taken shelter among the cedars, leaving their horses on the bench below, and, while some cattlemen pressed on ahead to join in the battle, Hawks took shelter behind a boulder and waited. His motive in coming south had been that of most of the cattlemen: a desire to clean up Coon Hole. As for killing Sundance Thorp, Hawks would leave that to the detectives who had blazed the way for their posse. They had intimated before starting that no outsiders were needed, if it came to a fight with the train robbers.

The firing had ceased now, only an occasional loud shout marking the progress the manhunters had made, but from the sound of their voices it was evident that the chase had led high up against the base of a precipice. Here, with the river on one side and the rock wall behind them, the train robbers had made a last stand, and, as evening was coming on, the detectives were closing in rather than risk an escape after dark. There was much shouting and challenging, even banter from those below, but Sundance and his men remained hidden. They were waiting – with their backs to the wall. A tense silence ensued, and to the cowmen down below it seemed as if the outlaws had vanished. Then, echoing from the cliff, there came the crack of a rifle, and a man slipped and fell from a ledge. Not until he began to fall was his presence suspected by those below, but he lay where he had fallen, dead. An aching silence followed, and then from either side stealthy forms crept up to the body. Not another shot was fired, and only when night had fallen did the sullen detectives return.

They brought the dead man with them, shot squarely between the eyes as he had thrust his head up over the last ledge, and, seeing the result of his foolhardiness, the rest of the manhunters had kept under cover until dark. The posse returned to the log house of the Kecks where they made themselves strictly at home, but rather than become involved in any controversy about the cattle, Hawks camped up on the bench, away from the mosquitoes. In the morning he rode down and looked across at the long ranch house, set under the brow of a hill, and already the cattlemen were assembling. The pursuit of the train robbers had proved a failure for the detectives, but now that the rustlers were scattered, the cowmen intended to sweep Coon Hole clean.

Bones was the man in the middle, giving the orders and doing the talking, and, when Hawks rode up, he immediately deputized him to cut Keck's herd for strays. But Bones was not the only one who had been watching for Hawks's coming. Penny came flying out to meet him.

'Oh, Clay,' she cried. 'Why haven't you been here? They're going to take all our cattle!'

'Sure,' he said. 'Why not?'

'Why not?' she echoed, her eyes big with anger. 'It's plain stealing, tha's all it is. And besides, we've sold half of them to Lord Abernathy, and it wouldn't be fair to him!'

She waved a dainty hand in the direction of an Englishman who was lingering nearby, smoking a pipe, but Hawks only gave him a glance. He was thinking of what he had suffered at Penny's hands.

'You worried yourself sick, didn't you,' he went on sarcastically, 'When your husband was stealing my steers? It wasn't right to steal them, was it? Well, this is part of the game when you run off and marry a cow thief, and you needn't look to me for any sympathy.'

'No, but listen, my good man,' broke in the Englishman excitedly, 'You don't realize the importance of this case. I bought these cattle in good faith, paying two thousand pounds for them, and, if you take them, I shall appeal to His Majesty's government.'

A loud guffaw came up from the group of listening cowmen, who had evidently heard this protest before, but Hawks did not join in the laugh.

'You'll have to appeal then, because these cattle have been stolen, and these gentlemen can claim everything in their brands.'

'But they're going to take them *all*, Clay!' cried Penny tearfully. 'Whether they have our brand or not! And David is a lord...'

'That makes no difference out here,' broke

149

in Hawks impatiently. 'We don't give a whoop if he's a king. If he's bought stolen stock, he's lost his money, that's all. What title can you show for these cattle?'

'Why ... I don't know what you mean,' answered Penny resentfully. 'But if you mean you're going to take them...?'

'We're not going to take a hoof that you can prove title to. Have you got any bills of sale?'

'Why, no. You see, Clay, Jim ran away and took all his papers with him. If it hadn't been for Lord Abernathy...' – she turned and smiled at him sweetly – 'I don't know what I'd have done.'

'Oh, it was nothing ... nothing,' Abernathy spoke up briskly, but Hawks saw the blush that mounted his blond cheeks and almost took pity on his innocence.

'I'll tell you, Mister Abernathy, or whatever your name is...'

'David Williams! And what is yours, pray?'

'Clayton Hawks,' he answered, and, as the Englishman offered his hand, the crowd guffawed again.

'Glad to meet you, Mister Hawks ... very glad, I'm sure. Now, what was it about the cattle?'

'If they've got your straight brand on them, you can claim them as your property. But if they've got some other man's brand, or if he can show where his brand has been

150

changed, we'll have to give them to him.'

'Fair enough,' declared the Englishman. 'Quite right, I'm sure. Would you mind if I go along?'

'Not at all,' returned Hawks, but, as Williams started into the house, Penny whispered a moment in his ear.

'I'm very sorry,' he said, turning gravely to Hawks, 'but perhaps I might better remain here. Disturbed conditions, you understand, and the little lady is such a brick...'

'All right,' nodded Hawks, and rode off grimly. He understood, better than the Englishman knew.

While the detectives were conducting a wary search of the high cliffs in an endeavor to locate Sundance and his gang, the posse of cattlemen threw a quick circle up the valley and gathered in Keck's herd. What few carried his straight brand were thrown back toward the ranch house, where the queen of the rustlers kept her lord, but every stray of any brand was ruthlessly cut and driven on over the hill to Payne's. Here most of the cattle ranged, attracted by the green grass and the springs that came out along the hillside, and without asking permission Hawks and his posse rounded them up and once more began to cut their strays.

But things had not gone well during their absence from the Payne ranch. Some of the gang had returned during the night, and, as a ghastly reminder of the power of the hidden outlaws, a man's body hung dangling from the corral gate frame. Hawks rode over to the house as soon as the roundup was well started and helped cut down the body. Whoever the man was, he had been suspected of intended treachery, and there he hung, a warning to all informers. But the significance of this hanging and the menace that lay behind it were lost on some of the posse. As Hawks rode past the gate, he heard an altercation in the house, where Mrs Payne was laying down the law. Four horses stood outside, and, knowing who rode them, Hawks dropped off and hurried up the path. Some of the posse had been loading up on whisky, and now they were making themselves objectionable.

At the clank of his spurs, Mrs Payne looked out the door and beckoned him in with a sigh. 'I'd just like to know,' she demanded, 'whether these men here can insult me, just because my husband is away. When Mister Payne hears of this, and of his daughters being insulted...'

Hawks looked at the four men, who were leering defiantly, and turned to the angry woman. 'No, Missus Payne,' he said, 'you won't be insulted. Can you get me a little breakfast?'

'Well, I can,' she flared back, 'if you'll keep these four brutes from calling through that door to my daughters, but you or no one else can come into my house...'

'All right,' he cut in, 'they won't do it.'

'Well, make them get out of here ... they've been sitting there for an hour, and I won't have my daughters insulted.'

'Did you gentlemen insult her daughters?' demanded Hawks after a silence, and the drunkest of the four spoke up. 'Insult, hell,' he jeered, 'her daughters are just like she is ... ain't she common to all these rustlers?'

The blush of shame that mantled Mrs Payne's cheeks went unnoticed in the fracas that followed. With a plunge Hawks caught the man by a leg and arm and hurled him out through the screen door, and then, rushing after him, he jerked him to his feet and kicked him down the path to the garden.

'Now you get on that horse,' he said, 'and beat it for Powder Springs. Never mind about your gun ... I'll keep it.'

He was a Hawks, like his father, and, when his righteous anger leaped up, weaker men felt it smite them like a blast. No man, drunk or sober, could say a word against any of the Payne women without answering to him for the insult. The drunken man rode away, his companions slinking after him, and Hawks mounted his own horse and spurred off. Rooster Raslem was right – Coon Hole was no place for a woman.

Chapter Fourteen

The herd of stolen cattle proved a hard bunch to handle when they came to the mouth of Irish Cañon. Besides the natural fears that the echoing cañon inspired in them, the cattle objected to leaving Coon Hole. It had often been commented upon that, while the mosquitoes were terrible there and the deer flies bled them like bloodsuckers, any horse or cow that had ever lived in Coon Hole was almost sure to return. Perhaps it was the grass, which was good the year around, or the winters, which were relatively mild, but there was something about Coon Hole that drew them like a magnet and made them loath to leave.

Hawks had proposed to drive the cattle up Vermilion Wash and thence through the badlands to his ranch, but as the posse was tired out and had nothing to eat but beef the route through Irish Cañon was preferred. Several differences of opinion had developed already before this particular question came up, and, finding himself outvoted, Hawks yielded to Bones who had begun to oppose him again. Now that his dream was fulfilled and they had cleaned out Coon

154

Hole, Bones was feverishly anxious to get away, and, when in the afternoon the posse of detectives rode past them, his fever became almost a panic.

It was the fear of the detectives, trained manhunters picked for their nerve, that had driven the Coon Hole rustlers into the hills, and, now that the detectives were gone, the gang would swarm down again, as they had on the evening before. The vision of that dead man, hung up by a pair of hobble straps to the frame of the Paynes' corral gate, was a sufficient incentive for speed, for it showed that the gang was desperate, but from the time they entered the cañon, the cattle refused to travel beyond a snail's pace. Darkness found them past Bear Spring, the only water in the cañon, but still miles away from Irish Lake, and it was well past midnight before they flogged them out of the portals and down to the water's edge to drink.

Irish Lake – a big lagoon, half snow pool, half mud hole – lay at the mouth of Irish Cañon, but, as the cattle spread out along its muddy shores, something startled them, and they broke for the hills. Once filled up with water and bedded down in the blue-stem grass, the herd would have been easier to hold, but when they were coaxed back to the edge of the boggy lake, the leaders refused to go in. Double guards were posted, all the horses were kept up with the herd, and the cattle were driven back inside the cañon, yet the same stubborn spirit that had animated them from the start still possessed them, and they milled restlessly about. As the night wore on, mysterious noises along the heights suggested the presence of horses, or even men, and the echoes of the herd's bawling, tossed back from the opposite cliff, gave an added impression of tumult.

Summoned to stand the last guard, Hawks found the cañon a pandemonium, cattle bellowing, men cursing, hoofs clacking against the rocks, and, as he took up his rounds, a boulder on the hillside gave way and fell crashing among the cedars. Even then he only half suspected that the heights were manned with rustlers, for rocks often fall of themselves, but as morning was coming on, a huge boulder up on the rim toppled over and came smashing down upon the herd. There was a volley of rifle shots, a chorus of shrill yells, and the stampede was almost upon him. Like one creature animated by one mind, the great herd leaped forward, rushing restlessly down the cañon toward Coon Hole, and, clutching at his saddle horn, Hawks let his horse scramble until he was safely out of their course. Others followed the cattle, cursing wildly, but the odds were too great, and Hawks did not even start. That avalanche could never be turned – not a hoof was ever brought back.

Well out in the open Hawks looked back at daybreak and saw the rustlers riding home over the ridge, and a few hours later all the cattlemen were around his fire, cooking strips of beef on a stick. What they said about Keck and his gang of cow thieves was no worse than what they had said before, only now every word carried the venom of a new hatred engendered by humiliation and defeat. They had suffered much at the hands of the rustlers, and at last they listened to Bones. Always before his tirades against Tel Payne and the cedar-snappers had been taken as a natural flow of spleen, but now, as he called for vengeance, they listened with sympathetic ears.

'I tell you, boys!' Bones shouted, 'there's only one way to stop this, and that is to get rid of Tel Payne. Then hire a good gunman to kill Keck and his rustlers, and we'll have some security on this range. I'm willing to take the lead, but one man can't do everything ... and I've got to have some money, too.'

'How much?' asked Dutch Henry who ran cattle east of Snake River and had lost several hundred head. 'And vat do you vant it for?'

'I want three thousand dollars,' declared Bones emphatically. 'Never mind what I want it for. You boys pass the hat and put the money in my hand, and I'll guarantee some results.'

'F'r instance?' queried another cowman cautiously. 'I'll ante, but I want to see one card.'

'The less you know, my friend,' replied Bones, smiling cannily, 'the less you'll be able to tell the judge. If some rustler should happen to be found dead and it was claimed that the cattlemen had done it, don't you see it's to your advantage not to know a thing about it ... not to know who done it, or nothing? Now I'm willing to take the lead, and I'll guarantee quick action, but I won't give no accounting for the money I spend, and I won't stand interfering with my plans. If there's any man here that thinks he can get action by appealing to the officers of the law, I'll chip in my full share and get behind him, but when a bunch of rustlers and cedar-snappers like them...'

'Dat's all right,' nodded Dutch Henry, ''ve know dat. Vat we vant to know is vere dis money vill go to ... in a general sort of vay?'

'It will go,' returned Bones, 'to hire an A-One cattle detective, to put the fear of God in their hearts. They don't care for the law, nor for the whole United States government, nor for *us* ... you saw what they done ... but you wait till Seldom Seen...'

'Aha,' smiled Dutch Henry, 'so dat's who! But Mister Bones ... can you get him?'

'Can I get three thousand dollars?' demanded Bones truculently. 'If I can, I can get Seldom Seen.'

'Just a minute,' interposed Hawks. 'Isn't this Seldom Seen a man that makes a business of killing?'

'He never killed a man yet,' declared Bones, 'that didn't have it coming to him ... plenty! You know how he works ... no fuss, no fireworks, just drifts in on the range like a cowboy but when he finds the men who are doing the stealing, he sends out his warning notices. If they go, well and good. If they don't ... well, he wipes 'em off the map. A sure shot ... never fails ... and, when he's cleaned up a district, he's gone ... no hanging around for blackmail. He's a man-killer, I admit it, but, gentlemen, I've met him, and, if there's anything he hates, it's a thief. He hunts cow thieves, he says, just like a wolfer hunts wolves, and he hates 'em like horny toads. Just his name is enough. If he comes into this district and sends out a few notices, there'll be the grandest scattering you ever saw ... he's sure a holy terror to rustlers.'

'I'm for him,' nodded Dutch Henry approvingly.

'He's up in Montana right now,' went on Bones. 'How about it ... shall I send and get him?'

'Not for me,' answered Hawks, but of all the responses his was the only objection, and Bones was at pains to ignore it.

'Now what about the money?' Bones inquired expectantly. 'They ain't a man here that hasn't lost ten times as much as it will take to make up three thousand dollars, and I'll start this right off by giving three hundred myself, besides doing all the work. If anything comes up, I'm the man that's responsible ... you fellers don't know nothing about it. All you know is that the Cattlemen's Protective Association has been formed, and I've been instructed to engage a detective. No checks ... you can pay me in cash. And here's another thing, boys... I'll hire this detective and give him his orders, but I can't have him working for me. That would give the whole game away. They'd be suspicious of all my men, and that ain't his way of working anyway. He'll come into this country like any other cowboy and take on wherever it seems best in order to get acquainted. He's got to get the confidence of these rustlers and the Wild Bunch before he can even begin to work, so if a feller comes up to your wagon and strikes you for a job...'

'But how vill ve know him?' demanded Dutch Henry eagerly.

'You won't know him, Henry,' grinned Bones. 'That's the best thing about Seldom Seen. He lives up to his name ... they don't nobody know him ... but you've heard what he's doing up in Montana. Half these rust-

lers down here have come out of Montana
to get away from Seldom Seen, and yet they
ain't a man among 'em that knows what he
looks like or anything about him. All they
know is he's a man that's liable to be anywhere ... or any *man*, as far as that goes.
He's liable to be the toughest damned rustler in the outfit or a peddler selling hairpins.
They don't know, Henry, who the hell he is,
and that's what gets 'em scairt.'

'Yes, but suppose, Mister Bones ... he
should ask *me* for a chob. Is he a beeg man,
now, or...?'

'I'll tell you,' broke in Bones. 'When I
close the deal with Seldom Seen, I'll give
him a kind of password. If any man, short or
tall, tackles one of you gentlemen for a job
and tells you your rope is dragging, that's
the password ... you give him the job. Your
rope is dragging! Understand?'

'Sure. I geev 'um,' agreed Dutch Henry
placidly, but Clay Hawks was not so
complaisant. He had been watching William
Bones as he unfolded his scheme, and he
saw that every detail had been considered.
This was no brand new idea, conceived on
the spur of the moment, but a well-laid plot
that Bones had been saving up. Hawks even
wondered, rather wildly, if Bones had not
abetted the stampede in order to gain his
point. But that, of course, was preposterous,
for Bones himself had lost cattle in this

disastrous ending of their raid. It was simply that he had availed himself of the present opportunity to strike while the iron was hot. Here were fifteen or twenty cattlemen, the biggest men in the district – the very committee, in fact, that he had chosen – robbed and flaunted by the Coon Hole gang, and what could be more natural than to spring this cherished scheme when they were all in a humor to accept it – to accept any scheme, in fact, that promised revenge? Yet the old antagonism that existed between them prompted Hawks to oppose the plan.

In the first place, he had no confidence in Bones's ability, to execute anything, no matter how carefully planned. Bones was long on schemes but short on accomplishments, when it came to handling men, and, after the tragic loss of his six hundred big steers, Hawks had sworn never to trust Bones again. He was a bungler and a blowhard, full of big schemes as a bag of wind, but utterly incapable of executing them, and always, in every scheme, there was something for William Bones – as, for example, this three thousand dollars. Bones had specified that there should be no accounting. And as far as the risk was concerned, it would fall, not on Bones, but on the man who actually hired Seldom Seen to work for him on his ranch. Bones would be out of it, holding the sack of money. All this passed through Hawks's mind as he watched the scheme take form and saw the cattlemen contributing to Bones's fund, but when it came to him, he pushed the hat aside and announced that he would not give a cent.

'But why not?' they demanded in a chorus.

'Well, in the first place,' began Hawks, 'I don't believe in hiring killers to do our dirty work for us. If it's got to be done, let's do it ourselves ... that's the way my dad always did it.'

'Yes, and if your old man was here,' Bones burst out harshly, 'he'd step in and take the lead, but when we call on you...'

'You called on me,' retorted Hawks, 'to take charge of this roundup, when we were cutting that Coon Hole herd, but after it was all done and we were out in the open, you started to tell me my business. I said we ought to go up through Vermilion Wash...'

'I knowed it!' pronounced Bones, nodding his head at the rest of them. 'He's just sore because he couldn't have his way. That's the reason he's opposed to this scheme.'

'I'm not opposed to your scheme!' Hawks answered sulkily. 'Go ahead, if you think you can cut it. But I'll never give a dollar to hire any man killed... I'm not up against it that bad. If any of these rustlers come up on Hawks Mesa and start stealing my cows, I figure I can handle them myself. And another thing Mister Bones, since you've brought the matter up, I'll never go into another scheme of yours, not since you lost me those six hundred steers.'

'Didn't I tell you?' demanded Bones, turning triumphantly to the other cattlemen. 'He's opposed to anything I bring up, no matter how good it is. But now, here, I want to ask you ... are we going to let one spoiled kid hold back this whole scheme I've proposed? I claim he's a hog in the manger. He ain't got the nerve to go into Coon Hole himself and clean it up like his father would've done, and at the same time he's so damned stubborn he won't chip in his share to hire Seldom Seen to do the business. W'y, gentlemen, I'll guarantee in six months' time...'

'Yes, you'll guarantee anything,' cut in Hawks, white with anger. 'But let me tell you something, Mister Bones. I took eight cowboys last fall and rode down into Coon Hole and cut out every Lazy B cow that they had, and, when Keck and his gang tried to make me give 'em back, I told 'em to come and get 'em. Did Keck back those cows? Not so that anyone would notice. But you, you damned pinhead, after putting me in charge, you were afraid you might have to fight, so you hollered your head off to take the herd up Irish Cañon, and you gentlemen know the rest. He did the same thing before, when I lost all my steers, and that's why I'm through with him... I'm done.'

'Yes, but Hawks,' reasoned Nagle, one of the Snake River cowmen, 'we've got to stick together or we're cleaned. And after they've cleaned us, they'll come up and clean you. So listen to me a minute. We don't want your money, or your name, or nothing. All we ask is that you come in on this deal with the rest of us and agree to co-operate, within reason. They ain't nobody going to be killed, or nothing of the kind... I'm opposed to all that myself ... but we'll get this Seldom Seen to send out a few notices, and that'll be all that's necessary. If it isn't, I'll come over and hire out for a cow-puncher, if you'll lead the gang of us into the Hole.'

He held out his hand, and Hawks could not refuse it, for Nagle and his father were old friends.

'All right, Mister Nagle,' he said, 'if that's the way it is, I accept.' But as the cattlemen crowded in to shake hands on the agreement, Bones spat and walked off.

Chapter Fifteen

William Bones was a man just the opposite of Hawks's idea of a gentleman. He was harsh and overbearing with a mean, sarcastic way of spitting out his envious thoughts, whereas Sam Hawks, Clay's father, although he was a fighter when aroused, had always been low-voiced and courteous. Sam Hawks's silences alone conveyed a suggestion of the fierce passions that struggled within him for utterance, and, when at last he spoke, it was always with the mastery of one who has conquered himself. He was a quiet man, and Hawks took after him. Yet at that meeting of the cattlemen, when Bones had called him a spoiled kid, he had allowed his smoldering rage to get the best of him. Since plain speaking was in order, he had called to their attention who it was that had bungled their plans. Yet in spite of his opposition Bones had had his own way, and Hawks had felt his gloating enmity. Now, three days later, after making his boast, Hawks found his two top horses gone.

He had told Bones and the cowmen, when they pressed him to join them, that he would take care of his stock himself, and, when he found the horses missing, he could imagine Bones's sarcastic laugh. The fact that two strange horses had been left in their place did little to placate his wrath, and, catching up two more, he took the trail at a lope, straight out across the mesa toward 'Dobe Town. The dew was still on the grass, so the tracking was easy, and he had a spare mount behind, but after he had passed down Rustler's Trail into the sink of the badlands, he had to slow down to a walk.

There were patches of hard ground that would barely show a track, and, now that he was down where the trailing was poor, the horse thief had begun riding in circles. Hawks traveled by landmarks to save wasting time, riding first to one gap and then to the other, instead of following the devious tracks, and, just as he had about decided that his man was heading for Coon Hole, two horsemen appeared, riding after him. They raised their right hands in the how sign of the Indians, and, when he beckoned them on, they rode up at gallop, both mounted on fresh Lazy B horses. One was stout and bullet-headed, with a bristling red mustache now generously powdered with alkali, and the other, who seemed the leader, was bleak-eyed and suspicious with a huge beak burned red by the sun.

'Mister Raslem?' he inquired, stepping off behind his horse.

Hawks stared in blank amazement. 'Ras-lem?' he repeated, and it flashed through his mind that these men were railroad detect-ives. They had followed the trail out from town. 'No, I'm Clayton Hawks. You're rid-ing two of my horses. What made you think I was Raslem?'

'We're looking for Raslem,' answered the hawk-nosed detective. 'Thought maybe you might be him.'

'I'm Clayton Hawks,' he assured him, and without being told he knew who it was he had been trailing. It was Rooster Raslem, the train robber – Raslem had stolen the horses to make his getaway. Without a thought that it might be some friend who had taken this liberty with his horse herd, Hawks had jumped into the saddle and started in pur-suit, determined to run down the thief. He had made his boast to Bones that he could look after his own, but this was something different again. Rooster Raslem was his friend, and as such he was welcome to the best two horses he had, but now he had come so far it was necessary for Hawks to keep on, lest the detectives suspect his sympathies.

'I'm looking for the man that stole my horses,' he said. 'What's this you say about Raslem?'

'He robbed the train again,' answered the stout man, grinning. 'Is this the trail you're following? Looks like he was heading south.'

'Yes. Believe it is,' agreed Hawks, suddenly remembering Raslem's cave. 'Come on, he's got my two horses.'

'And a horse load of loot,' added the fat man, grinning again as he fell in beside Hawks. 'Pretty slick, you've got to admit. Got him a sawed-off shotgun like express messengers use and walked up to the through car at Green River. We've been putting on extra guards since that robbery last week, so everybody thought Raslem would stay away. Tapped three times on the door, and, when the messenger opened up, he jumped in just as the train was pulling out. First we heard about the robbery, he had stopped the train near Powder Springs, along about two in the morning, and the messenger gave the alarm. Raslem had spent the whole two hours going through that express safe while the train was coming east to where his horses were. How's that for iron nerve?'

Hawks nodded, his eye on the trail. 'He's got a big start,' he suggested.

'Ever been through this country?' called back the leader who was riding ahead. 'Well, see if you can follow this trail.'

'All right,' assented Hawks, and then he headed the chase in pursuit of his renegade friend.

Having ridden from Powder Springs since daylight that morning, the detectives were saddle-sore and weary, and the glare of the sun on the desolate flats made the trailing doubly difficult. Yet Hawks was determined to show no lack of zeal, and he followed the faint horse trail for miles.

Once down in Vermilion Wash the tracks became plain again, plunging at last into Vermilion Cañon, and, still leaning low as if hot on the trail, Hawks led them past the cave at a gallop. No man would have suspected a robber's cave in that stark cliff, but from the tracks Hawks knew Raslem was there for he saw that the horses were running free, having been stripped of their plunder and rigging. When their first mad dash was ended, they dropped back to a trot, finally stopping at the creek for a drink. As the sun was swinging low, Hawks saw them in the distance, feeding peacefully on a grassy flat. There were maneuvers and stealthy approaches, anxious searching on every side for some sign of the vanished train robber, but as darkness came on, Hawks rode in and caught his horses, and they camped where they were for the night.

It was crowding friendship pretty far for Rooster Raslem to steal Clay Hawks's horses and put him to all the trouble of this chase, but, now that he had them back, Hawks let the matter pass, for Raslem would have his joke. When Hawks rode down to see him in a week or so, he could imagine his cackling laugh, and, after he had given the full account of his exploit, Hawks would get the latest gossip from Coon Hole. Nor had he forgotten that it was Raslem who had informed him of the treachery of Jim Keck and his Texans, and before the affair was ended, he might need further favors from this man who had raided his pasture. So he rode back to his ranch, leaving the detectives to beat the brush in search of the elusive Raslem.

Another big posse followed hot on the trail, for Rooster Raslem had made a big haul, and before they had finished the cedar-snappers of Coon Hole were driven far back into the hills. Some of the boldest of the posse even ventured up the trails that led over the summit of Black Mountain, but a week of futile search only strengthened their opinion that the robbers could never be run down. There were mountains beyond mountains, trails and hold-outs without end, rivers and cañons that could never be crossed and, although no one was killed, the detectives knew full well that the country was nothing less than a deathtrap. Every cliff and cedar stump was a potential ambush.

They came back by way of the Hawks ranch to return the horses they had borrowed, and those who would talk gave Hawks to understand that a change in their tactics had been decided upon – such pursuits were worse than useless. Some even hinted vaguely that they had decided to work from within, slip men in and have them join the gang, but one and all they handed the palm to Raslem, even questioning if he would ever be caught. Sundance Thorp and his gang had formed the dangerous habit of riding into town for a big drink, but Rooster Raslem was a man who had no bad habits to betray him and a man who worked alone. After a job he disappeared, as if the earth had swallowed him – no one knew where he went or whence he came. Hawks listened, saving it up for Raslem.

Stray men began to drop in shortly after the posse had left, ostensibly cowpunchers looking for a job, but Hawks had developed a keen eye for detectives, having seen nothing else for a month. He informed them all politely that he was full-handed for the present, and they rode on regretfully, going south. The range branding had begun when, one morning after breakfast, a cowpuncher who was actually a cowpuncher rode up. Hawks knew *him*, too, by the bow of his legs and the way he stepped down off his horse. After eating a hearty meal with the Lazy B cowboys, he ambled over to Hawks and applied for a job. He was a big, coarse-featured man, a mountain of elemental strength, and something about his nose and the shape of his lips made Hawks suspect a little Indian blood. His nose had the peculiar book and the broadness that is found among the Blackfeet and Sioux, and his lips, thrusting out, looked as if he had kissed a lamppost when the iron was black with frost. Only his twinkling eyes redeemed him from being an abysmal brute – that, and his air of absolute competence. He looked like a promising hand.

'What's the chance for a job?' he inquired.

'Well, I don't know,' replied Hawks. 'Can you ride?'

'Anything that wears hair ... I can ride him,' he said, and the cowpunchers standing nearby began to smile.

'All right!' grinned Hawks. 'I can't ride much myself, and these boys are in about the same fix, but we've got a horse out here, and any man that can ride him will come pretty close to getting a job.'

'Bring him out,' returned the 'puncher. 'I'll tame him.'

'Catch up T-Bone,' ordered Hawks, and they waited, while the wrangler brought up the herd.

'Let me snare him,' called the stranger after old T-Bone, a gaunt roan, had evaded their ropes. 'That's where I shine, boys, twirling the catgut.'

He took down a rawhide reata as slender as a clothesline from the horn of his double-rigged saddle and ran, laughing, into the round corral. All his awkwardness had left him, and, when he shot out his trailing loop, it went with the precision of a rifle bullet. T-Bone ducked his head and cringed, but the rope settled about his neck, and he came out as meekly as a deacon. The rest of the horses were released, and, while the stranger cinched on his saddle, the Lazy B boys mounted the fence.

'Any word for your folks?' they shouted at him cheerfully. 'Hey, think what you've got to live for!'

'Yes, tell 'em I died riding him,' answered the 'puncher.

He stepped up into the saddle with the same stealthy grace that he had shown when he whirled his rope, and, as he jerked away the gunny sack that had served him for a blind, he slapped it across T-Bone's face. T-Bone rose up on his hind legs, pawing the air and squealing viciously, and, when he hit the ground, he threw a half turn, then, grunting and squirming, he leaped stiff-legged across the corral and fetched up against the fence with a crash. There was a flurry of biting and kicking as he came out of the dust cloud, and then T-Bone rose up as if to fall backward, but the rider, sitting limber, seemed to poise in one stirrup, and the prize bucker of the Lazy B gave it up. After bucking across the corral again, he seemed suddenly to lose heart and stood trembling while the stranger got off.

'Nice little horse,' he said, grinning up at Hawks, and the cowboys yelled in chorus. Next to seeing a man thrown, they liked to see a broncho ridden, and they looked at the boss expectantly. But although his horse had been ridden, Hawks did not yield on the moment to the unspoken demands of the cowpunchers. The times were more than troubled, and, before he hired this man, he wanted to know who he was. Lots of rustlers were good riders – and railroad detectives, too – and he didn't want another Jim Keck on his hands.

'Come over to the house,' he said. 'I have to be kind of particular who I hire.'

The cowboy trailed along behind Hawks, as nerveless as an Indian, rolling his eyes at the others as he passed. Already he was a favorite with the Lazy B boys by virtue of his droll gift of silence. He seemed to speak with silence as other men resort to words – as if words, to his genius, were superfluous. A mere roll of the eyes, a pouting of his thick lips, and they joined in his silent laughter. Even his bow-legged walk, like the ambling of a bear, was indescribably ludicrous, and Hawks knew that the roundup would go better on account of his antics and jokes.

'You're a good rider,' he observed when they were back in his den that served both for office and bedroom. 'What name do you go by at present?'

'Oh ... er ... John Hicks,' grinned the cowboy. 'Yes, John Hicks, that's right. What was *your* name back in Texas?'

'Never been there. They call me Clay Hawks out here. Did you say you came from Texas?'

'No, sir, I did not. I'm from up north ... up in Montana. How about it ... do I get that job?'

'That depends,' temporized Hawks. 'I can use a good rider, but how are you with the running iron? Know how to write your name?'

'That's one thing I never monkey with,' replied the cowboy soberly. 'I won't steal calves for nobody.'

'That's all right,' returned Hawks. 'This outfit is on the square. You don't happen to be a detective?'

A sudden change, like wind across a lake, passed over the cowboy's rugged face, and he glanced about uneasily. 'What give you that idee?' he asked.

'Well, you look like one,' stated Hawks, following up this shot in the dark. 'Maybe you're down here hunting for train robbers?'

'Nope, your rope's dragging there, pardner. I'm a damned good broncho fighter, but train robbers are out of my line.'

'What is your particular line?' inquired Hawks, after a silence

The stranger closed one eye. 'I'm a

broncho fighter,' he said, and waited.

Hawks looked at him dubiously, feeling that something was expected of him yet puzzled as to what it might be. 'Well, what is it?' he demanded impatiently.

'I said *your rope was dragging,*' returned the broncho fighter significantly.

Suddenly Hawks nodded his head. 'Oh, I understand,' he said 'Well, that makes a difference. All right, you get your job.'

Chapter Sixteen

As he looked at this man who had informed him that his rope was dragging, Hawks felt certain there had been some mistake. Either Bones had bungled again and hired the wrong man, or the stranger had just picked up the phrase. He was too good-natured, too jovial and friendly, to be Seldom Seen, the killer.

'Er ... did Bones send you out here?' Hawks asked, lowering his voice.

The cowpuncher shook his head. 'I don't work that way.'

'Well, how do you work? Are you the man that Bones sent for? I believe you said you came from Montana?'

'Yes, I'm the man, but Bones didn't send

me out here. I don't take orders from no man. I go where I please and use my own judgment. Ever see one of my little signs?'

He drew out a cigarette paper and the stump of a pencil that he wet as he moved over to the table. Then with the ponderous care of one who writes little he drew a capital S. The upper prong he doubled back in the shape of a serpent's head, with a forked tongue and a dot for an eye, and on the lower end he added a little curlicue to represent the tail of a rattlesnake. Then across the square of paper he spelled out laboriously the letters: SELDOM SEEN. Each e, by a dot, was transformed into a serpent's head exactly like the head of the S, and the S of Seen was likewise embellished to represent a rattlesnake, striking.

'How's that?' he inquired, and, when Hawks had admired it, he rolled it into a cigarette. 'This is between you and me,' he confided. 'Nobody else knows who I am. I'd like to stay here for a while until I get acquainted with the Wild Bunch, and then I'll throw in with them. When I pick out the bad ones, I'll send 'em a cigarette paper, and they'll leave like a bat out of hell. I reckon you've heard of me down here?'

'Yes, your fame has preceded you,' Hawks answered dryly.

Seldom Seen glanced at him shrewdly. 'You're the first man that ever spotted me for a detective. That's why I decided to come through. I've got a few things I'd like to leave here for a while ... have you got some place that's safe?'

'Bring 'em in,' returned Hawks, and, as the killer tramped out, he shook his head and sighed. By some strange fatality all of Bones's evil chickens seemed to come to his ranch to roost. First Keck and his Texans, and now the man hired to kill them. Rooster Raslem had been right when he said that, in this country, there was no room for an honest man. All the forces of evil seemed to be conspiring together to pull Hawks down with the rest. First he had befriended Raslem himself for old time's sake and because he was a good man gone wrong, and then his own fiancée had been snatched by a man he would otherwise have killed. Now he found himself harboring a hired assassin undoubtedly instructed to kill Keck. The fates were whirling him on toward his destiny, whatever that might be.'

Seldom Seen came back, grinning, a beaded war bag under his arm. 'How's that?' he gloated, unwrapping a knocked-down carbine and connecting the gleaming parts. 'Ever seen one of these before? It's the latest thing out, one of the new model Thirty-Thirtys, the only gun like it in the country. I'd like to have you keep this for a while.'

Hawks looked the carbine over, and, as he

glanced down the fine sights, he wondered how many men it had killed. Yet so perfectly was it made that, in spite of his revulsion, he thrilled as it touched his cheek. It was a masterpiece of gun-making, and Seldom Seen surveyed it proudly.

'You just can't miss 'em with that.'

'No, I suppose not,' assented Hawks. 'Well, every man to his own taste ... we'd better keep this out of sight.' He lifted two boards in the corner of the room and thrust the bundle under the house. 'All right now,' he resumed, 'we'll just forget this, Mister Hicks. I'm not much for killing myself. Any time you want it, you'll have to see me first. I never leave my door unlocked.'

'Yours truly,' saluted Hicks, and went swinging out of the door to ride after the boys on the roundup.

Hawks watched Hicks curiously for the next two or three weeks, still looking for the killer blood to come out, but off on the range or telling stories in the bunkhouse he was always the carefree cowpuncher. He chose out of preference the worst horses in the cavvy, and every morning, as he came bucking out the gate, there were whoops of joy from the cowboys. When they were idling at the ranch, he would engage in feats of strength or run bow-legged races across the horse lot, and at night howls of laughter from the pitch-dark bunkhouse would rouse Hawks from his sleep. As a practical joker Hicks yielded the palm to no man, and yet he was a cold-blooded murderer. He had made a name of terror all through the Northwest, but he slept and ate like a bear. Hawks wondered if all the moralists were wrong, for there was no mark of Cain on his brow. Only his fearless resolution as he walked up to a fighting horse gave an inkling of the real Seldom Seen. He was a man of iron, cast in the heroic mold of a Lancelot or a Richard the Lionhearted, and now, in a later day when manslaughter was a crime, he was working out his belated destiny.

Things went well with the range branding. Hawks already had an increase after the loss that had almost left him bankrupt, yet as soon as the detectives left the rustlers undisturbed, they began to menace his upper range. Twice within the three weeks they had ridden to Powder Springs and taken the town by storm, but since they had bounced gold pieces off the bar and sowed the town with easy money no hurry call was sent to the detectives. Yet all of this meant trouble, and, having in mind the struggle to come, Hawks rode down across his lower range. The broad valley of the Alkali was empty of cattle. In that silence only the antelope stood at graze, but it was still the Hawks range and Hawks rode it with a jealous eye, noting the grass that was there to feed his cows. And one evening, just at dusk, he spurred his horse down Vermilion Cañon and looked up at Raslem's cave.

A head, no longer shaggy, thrust out of the hole to greet him, and, nimble and joyous as a chipmunk, Rooster came stepping down over the rocks and beckoned him up to his cave. Hawks untied a sack of newspapers from the back of his saddle and climbed up to the now familiar robber's cave. There were new pictures on the wall, a sawed-off shotgun in one corner, and Raslem cackling with laughter. Hawks wondered in some bitterness what it was that made him happy while honest men were downhearted and grim. This train robber and Seldom Seen were the only men in the country who knew how to crack a smile.

'Heh. Heh. Lose any horses?' inquired Raslem mischievously. 'Say, you sure came down through here like the clatter wheel of hell ... didn't you know who it was you were trailing?'

'Well, I might've,' admitted Hawks, 'but a man in my position has got to be careful about his friends. I was hoping you were going to reform.'

'Nope! One more shot!' spoke up Rooster resolutely. 'One more, and I'm fixed for life. Say, lemme see them papers! How much did they say get? Eight nothing ... I got forty

... thousand ... dollars! Ain't it fierce how these papers will publish such lies? "Eight thousand in unsigned bank notes!"'

He read on impatiently, throwing down one paper after the other until finally he kicked them all into a corner.

'Nothing but bunk,' he declared. 'I got more lone-handed than Sundance and his whole gang combined and look at the scrap they had. A man don't git no credit when he does a clean job ... all the newspapers want is some sensation.'

'Never mind,' consoled Hawks. 'You'll have that much less to get away from when you start to live down your past. This publicity that Sundance gets and having his picture in all the papers are going to get him killed, some of these days.'

'He's a good kid,' defended Raslem, 'but I don't like the crowd he runs with ... some of those cedar-snappers are going to squeal on him, sure.'

'Yes, and about one more big drunk in Powder Springs and he'll think it's the Custer massacre. Those detectives have got a special car.'

'Has he been to town again?' exclaimed Raslem in dismay. 'He's running hog-wild, that's all. Sure them officers will get him. They'll shoot him in the back just to grab that twenty thousand dollars. I see they's ten thousand up on me!'

'You'd better quit,' coaxed Hawks. 'You've got plenty already ... what do you want to go back and get killed for? They'll be watching for you next time...'

'Let 'em watch,' nodded Raslem. 'I'll show 'em ... you wait ... and this time I fly the coop. Three times and I'm out. I'll have my ticket for South America, and, if you ever come down there, say around Buenos Aires, you'll find me living like a king. I'm going to get me a big ranch and one of them pretty little Spanish girls and every day I'm going to order sowbelly and beans for dinner and throw it across the room to the dogs. I've got more cash right now than you and Bones combined, and here you are, trying to get me to quit. You're jealous, that's what's working on *you!*'

'Sure,' agreed Hawks. 'It'd make anybody jealous to see you living in this dog hole, and the last time I was here I reckon a mess of pork and beans would have gone pretty damned good.'

'Oh, hell,' argued Raslem, 'that ain't no way to look at it. Don't every business have its drawbacks? I may run out of grub when old man Payne has a tantrum, but you don't find me out standing night guard. And when I get real lonely, I dig up a thousand dollar bill and think what it's going to buy me. No, they's drawbacks to everything, but I'm playing this game to win ... and I'm going to

184

do it, too.'

He jerked his head like a rooster looking up for a hawk, and Hawks smiled good-naturedly, for he had learned when Raslem was set. He was a man who, all his life, had dared to stand alone, and, if he was crowded too far, he would fight.

'Well, what's the news?' Hawks asked. 'Did you get that tobacco I left for you? I thought you always stayed in your hole.'

'Don't you think it!' boasted Raslem. 'I do my traveling nights and know more than some people that travel daytimes. You think I don't know what's going on, eh?' He rolled a cigarette and cocked his head at Hawks. 'That's a right comical broncho buster you've got!'

'Yes,' answered Hawks, smiling wisely.

'Funny stories he tells ... that's a good one about Simpson.' And Raslem exploded with laughter.

'Simpson?' repeated Hawks.

Raslem tittered mischievously. 'Now, you see!' he gloated. 'You don't know it.'

'Maybe *you* don't,' suggested Hawks. 'Before you laugh your damned head off, maybe you'd better give me a sketch.'

'I'll go you,' returned Raslem. 'It's a good one. There was a hobo down south, broke into a feller's home, and got away with a coat, but when he put it on, it had a square collar, like preachers and bishops wear.

Well, winter was coming on and hoboes can't be too particular, so he put it on when he came to the next town, but the first door he battered on, instead of sicking the dog on him, the lady of the house invited him in. Spread him out a clean white tablecloth, gave him canned pears and everything, and then here comes the yaller-legged chicken. This coat that he stole had belonged to some minister, and the good lady took him for a preacher. That night they bedded him down in the spare front bedroom and killed him another chicken the next day, but the hell of it was he didn't know enough Scripture to live up to the preacher's part. He stalled around as long as he could, but the good lady kept after him, and one day she put him in a hole.

"'Brother Jinkins,' she says, "you know the Bible so well, won't you tell me what's your favorite verse?"

"'Well, sister,' he says, "I love the whole Bible. I got no favorite verse."

"'Yes, but Brother Jinkins,' she says, "you mustn't look down on us poor country folks, just because, we ain't educated like you be. They's all kinds of wonderful characters in the Bible ... won't you tell me which one you like the best?"

"'Well,' says the hobo, "I admire 'em all, of course, but of all them Bible characters the one I admire the most is that long-haired feller, Simpson."

"'Oh, Brother Jinkins," she says, "you must be joking me ... or perhaps you refer to Samson?"

"'No ... Simpson!" says the hobo. "I guess I know who I mean ... the man that took the jaw-bone of a mule and knocked the hell out of a thousand Philadelphians!"'

'That sounds more like one of yours,' suggested Hawks. 'I don't believe my broncho fighter would tell it.'

'Well, name me one!' challenged Raslem. 'That was a good one on old Bones, eh? But, say, didn't you hear him tell that? Well, I don't give a whoop whether you believe it's his or not ... you just ask him if it ain't when you git back. Old Bones, he died and went to heaven, but when he came to the gate, Saint Peter stopped him and asked him for his name.

"'William Bones," he says, "of Powder Springs, Wyoming."

"'Just a moment," says Saint Peter, "till we look up your record." And he called for the Recording Angel.

"'What's the matter?" says Bones. "What are you looking for?"

"'It's the rule," says Saint Peter, "that no one is admitted here unless they've done two-bits' worth of good with their money. What's the record of William Bones, Gabe?"

"'I find here," says the Angel Gabriel,

"where he gave five cents to a little boy ... and here's ten cents he gave to an old woman."

"'Well, go on," says Saint Peter, "ain't there any more?"

"'That's all, Peter," says the Angel Gabriel.

"'Well, well," says Saint Peter, "what do you think we'd better do?"

"'Aw, give him back his fifteen cents," says Gabe, "and tell him to go to hell!'"

Rooster Raslem laughed long and loud at this slam at old Bones, but Hawks paused at a disquieting thought.

'What does Hicks know about Bones?' he asked.

'Why, for Christ's sake!' exclaimed Rooster, 'didn't you hear about that, either? He tackled Bones for a job when he came through Powder Springs, and Bones offered him thirty a month. Thirty dollars a month for the best broncho rider in the country! I know where he can get a hundred.'

'Where's that?' demanded Hawks.

Rooster cocked his head saucily. 'In Coon Hole,' he said, 'working for Keck.'

'Oho,' observed Hawks, looking grim.

'Don't you never think,' went on Raslem, 'that them rustlers don't know all about him. They know more about him than you do. And the first time he goes to town, they're going to get him drunk and toll him down to Coon Hole to ride Indian Killer. Do you think he can do it, Clay?'

'I don't know, and I don't care,' Hawks answered shortly, but he began to see through Seldom Seen's game. 'Who told you all this?' he inquired.

'A little bird,' winked Raslem. 'You must think I'm a damned fool. But I know ... don't you worry about that. They ain't nothing goes on in this part of the country that I couldn't tell you, if I wanted to, and at the same time, Clay, they ain't another man in the country but you that knows where Rooster's cave is. They all think I'm hiding out in 'Dobe Town. You can't never tell which one of them bad eggs is a detective. I hear you folks have sent for Seldom Seen.' He shot this out quickly, to take Hawks by surprise, and sat watching him with beady eyes.

'You hear lots of things,' Hawks answered calmly.

'They's no use bluffing,' declared Raslem. 'The gang knows all about it, and the first damned detective that they ketch in Coon Hole they're going to hang him, like they did that other fellow.'

'What do you mean?' demanded Hawks. 'Was that man we found hanging there...?'

'Sure! That feller you cut down was a detective. He thought he had 'em fooled and was slipping out with information, but when that posse came in, they jest grabbed Mister Detective and hung him with a pair of hobbles.'

'They're a hard outfit,' observed Hawks, shaking his head.

'Yes, and another thing,' went on Raslem, a threatening gleam coming into his eyes, 'the first man that Seldom Seen kills, they're going to clean up on you and Bones. They know who's behind this, so you want to hunt your hole before you turn that wolf loose on the boys.'

'You can tell your friends,' returned Hawks, 'that there'll be no dirty work done for me ... by Seldom Seen or anybody else ... but if they want to avoid trouble, the best way to do it is to lay off stealing my cattle. I can kill my own snakes, and the first man that raids Hawks Mesa will have me to deal with personally.'

'Oh, they ain't *my* friends,' protested Raslem. 'Sundance and my bunch don't mix up with them rustlers much. I just thought I'd let you know. Who was it you had in mind ... Keck?'

'Keck or any of them. I've got a bellyful of this stealing and...'

'Have you heard the latest?' gloated Raslem. 'The son-of-a-bitch has got Pearl into trouble, and they're sending her off to Denver. It was her mother found it out, but Pearl tried to lie out of it to save him. Ain't it simply hell the way these women fall for him? How come you never killed him, Clay?'

Raslem leaned over closer, looking up into Hawks's face with a sly, insinuating smile, but Hawks pushed him roughly away.

'Rooster,' he said, 'you're a regular old woman. Every time I come down here, you tell me a lot of stuff that pretty near makes me sick. I'm going now, and I'm never coming back.'

'Yes, you are coming back,' asserted Raslem, 'because you need me in your business, just as much as I need you in mine. And don't you ever think that this gossip ain't important, because them women are running Coon Hole. Missus Payne has got more influence with Sundance Thorp than me and the whole 'Dobe Town gang, and as for Keck's wife ... they's going to be a killing down there if she don't let upon that lord.'

'Oh, the lord, eh?' repeated Hawks, intrigued in spite of himself by the smile in Raslem's beady eyes. 'He seemed like a pretty good fellow.'

'Well, he's rich,' conceded Raslem, 'and I guess he's a genuwine lord ... came through here on a big game hunt ... but the way they've flimfammed that bloody, blooming Englishman seems to indicate he's shy on gray matter. And he drinks this danged Scotch whisky! But, anyway, he came through here, and his guide went off and left him, so he stopped at the Keck place, and, bah Jove, it looked so good with the cut glass and decanters that the lord decided to stay. Never occurred to him that everything wasn't all right ... he thought all Westerners were outlaws, anyway ... and when his next remittance came due, he paid the whole ten thousand dollars for a half share in Keck's Heart brand. Now he's stranded, dontcherknow, until his next check comes in, and all he does is make love to that woman. If Keck wasn't so busy collecting hair for that scalp lock...'

'Is that all you can talk about?' broke in Hawks.

'Well, if he wasn't, he'd see what his wife is up to. She's trying to snare that Englishman, that's what she's trying to do, and then get him to run Keck off, but Missus Payne says his lordship ain't got the nerve ... you know she and Missus Keck don't hitch. But when them two get to spatting, it's the pot and the kettle, because Missus Payne has gone wrong with Sundance ... but you can't blame her, Clay, living there with them outlaws. I guess they've all gone wrong.'

'All?' repeated Hawks, rising swiftly to his feet. 'You don't mean ... not Mary, too!'

His whole face had changed, and at the look in his eye Raslem blanched and backed hastily away. 'Whit's the matter?' he complained, and then with a loud laugh he clapped Hawks on the shoulder. 'Mary!' he cried. 'Hell, no don't you never think it! You could no more put your hand on Mary Payne than you could on a broncho colt. But what's the matter, Clay ... where are you going?'

'I'm going back home,' answered Hawks, 'to get away from your damned dirty talk.'

Chapter Seventeen

Since Seldom Seen had come to the ranch, Hawks had stayed away from the bunk-house, nor had Seldom Seen tried to expand their acquaintance after making his identity known, but when his month was up, he came with another 'puncher and asked Hawks for his time. Hawks wrote out their time checks and watched them ride off toward Powder Springs and a big drunk. That was the regular routine, but when they came back, Hawks knew that something had happened. They had been gone a week – and they rode in from the south, instead of on the trail from town. A few days later, when the boys were out with the wagon, Seldom Seen circled back and rode up to the house.

'Well, boss,' he said, when they had retired to Hawks's office, 'I went down among 'em last week, and you might say I'm a member of the gang. That feller I was with is their lookout with this outfit. I spotted him the first day you took me on, and, when we got to Powder Springs, the whole gang was there, a-rollin' 'em high and handsome. We throwed right in with 'em, and, after I'd rode a couple of bronc's, they invited me down to Coon Hole. There's the wildest bunch of *hombres* I ever went up against, and that Injun Killer is the wickedest horse, but I was just drunk enough to ride him right, and it left me ace high with the gang. I not only rode him, but I emptied a bottle of whisky and tipped my hat to the ladies while he was acting up his best. Then he ran into the fence and broke his neck.'

He grinned and sat down by the table.

'And drunk!' he went on. 'Never was so drunk in my life. We all got drunk, and stayed drunk. And after we'd drunk up all the booze at the Payne place, we went down and camped with Keck. There's one of the prettiest riders I ever saw in my life ... and that black feller can ride, too ... but the best man among 'em was afraid to fork Indian Killer, so there I was again, ace high. But lawdy, lawdy, what they was going to do to Seldom Seen, if he ever showed his head in Coon Hole!'

He laughed good-naturedly, and began to draw a serpent on a cigarette-paper from his book.

'More men down there,' he said, 'with

rewards on their heads than in all the rest of the West. I counted eleven in one bunch worth five thousand or better, and Sundance Thorp is worth twenty.'

'Yes, but Sundance Thorp, my friend, is in the train-robbing business, and we're not worrying about him.'

'I know, I know,' nodded Seldom Seen. 'But I'm talking about rustlers, too. That black feller is shy one ear, and unless I'm badly mistaken there's a reward for him down in Texas.

'"Curly Bill," I says, when we were all drunk together, "how come you lost that ear?"

'"Well, I'll tell you, mistah," he says. "I had a little difficulty with a black man back in Texas."

'"And then what?" I says. "Did he bite ye?"

'"Out went an eye," he says, "and off come an ear." And he made a kind of pass at my eye. Believe somebody told me he and Keck had worked together, but I was too danged drunk to remember. Stealing cattle along the Mexican line.'

'I don't doubt it,' nodded Hawks. 'They're all fugitives from justice ... came in over that Robbers' Trail ... but I'll tell you, Mister Hicks, you're working for William Bones, so you'd better talk this over with him.'

'No, I'm telling this to you,' answered the cowboy stubbornly. 'To hell with old Bones

... I don't like him. But I've been watching you, Mister Hawks, and you're a man that can keep his mouth shut, so I'll tell you what I've got in mind. There'll never be an end to rustling in this country until that whole Coon Hole gang is wiped out. No use in killing a few cow thieves on the side. It's the leaders we've got to git. All right ... here's how to git 'em. You know that bank in Powder Springs? It'd've been robbed long ago if there was anything there worth the taking. Well, make it worth the trouble and sure as God made little apples the gang will ride in and tap it. Then I'll tip you off when the robbery is about to take place, and you can wipe out the whole damned outfit. Shoot 'em down when they're right in the act ... all I ask is my half of the rewards.'

'You'd better talk to Bones,' suggested Hawks.

'No, I'm talking to you,' replied the killer insistently. 'What's the matter ... don't you think it will work?'

'Why, yes, I believe it would,' returned Hawks impersonally. 'But let me tell you something, Mister Hicks. I don't approve myself of the kind of work you're doing ... if I had my way they'd never have hired you ... so there's no use talking to me about these killings. What you've told me today will never go any further, but you're better discussing the details with Bones.'

'He'll blab it!' objected Hicks. 'Old Bones talks too much, but at the same time we've got to use him. You see, it's this way with those train robbers ... they're suspicious of everybody, and, if they ever thought that this bank robbery was being planted, they'd never come near the place. Well, have a piece in the newspaper that the Powder Springs Bank has been taken over by Bones, and that he's made a deposit of thirty or forty thousand to increase the capital stock and all that. The Paynes take the *Rawlins News* ... so put it in there ... and then make old Bones put up the forty thousand dollars, because them fellers have got ways of finding out. Put the money in the bank and they're going to find out about it. You don't need to worry about that. And then, when I tip you off, put about twenty regular gunmen where they can rake that street the whole length. Right there in one night you can clean out this nest of rustlers and make a lot of money besides. All I want is my half of the rewards.'

'Very nicely thought out,' observed Hawks, still politely, 'but I'll tell you, Mister Hicks, I've had troubles with Bones, and I don't want to have any more. He seems to make it a life study how to get me into some jackpot every time I have anything to do with him. So you can count me out of it, and, if you'll take my advice, you'll keep away from Bones entirely.'

'Huh? I wouldn't trust Bones to pack guts to a bear,' spoke up Hicks with deep disgust, 'only I've got to use the old bastard. Them Coon Hole cedar-snappers would ride a thousand miles to rob one of his banks of ten dollars. I've just got to use him, that's all.'

'I've always thought,' said Hawks as this hired sharpshooter fell silent, 'that old Bones steered you out here to my ranch. That's the way he always works. And when Coon Hole discovers that I've been sheltering Seldom Seen...'

'Don't you worry, Mister Hawks,' replied Hicks reassuringly, 'they'll never find out who I am. I'm the slickest stock detective that ever sat in on the game, and I never rat on my friends. If you treat me white, you'll never regret it. Only I wish you'd come in on this scheme. Won't do it, eh? Well, I'll have to talk to Bones, then.'

'He'll ditch you,' predicted Hawks. 'I know him.'

Seldom Seen rode into town, and a few days later William Bones called a meeting of the cowmen. What took place then Hawks only knew from hearsay as he made it a point not to attend, but he learned in a general way that Bones had stated the proposition as if it had originated with him, and he had also distinctly specified that, in return for the risks he would take, all the reward money was to go to him. The Cattlemen's Protective Association was so taken with the scheme that they had agreed to everything and given Bones carte blanche. When their services were required, they would be there to do the killing. Meanwhile, Bones was authorized to go ahead and make all the necessary arrangements.

The next issue of the *Rawlins News* contained a legal notice that the Bank of Powder Springs had changed hands, and that all moneys due were payable to William Bones who had assumed the full management of the bank. And then the following week, Hawks found the planted notice that was intended to lure the outlaws to their deaths. It was an article highly laudatory of William Bones, the new president of the Powder Springs-Bank, the capital stock of which had been increased to one hundred thousand dollars of which fifty thousand dollars had been paid up. A new era of prosperity was predicted for Custer County as well as for the Powder Springs Bank, as the name of William Bones was a guarantee of sound business management as well as of ample financial backing.

Hawks put the paper down with a muttered curse – how old Bones did luxuriate in petty treachery. If ever there was a man fitted for treason, stratagems, and spoils, it was Bones, and yet he always failed. A thousand times Hawks had flushed with humiliation as he remembered how Jim Keck had outwitted them and a thousand times again he had cursed his own weakness in yielding the leadership to Bones. Even now he could not remember by what specious arguments the discredited ranch manger had persuaded him to yield, but from that day when they rode up and demanded a range count of Keck, everything in his life had gone wrong. Face to face with the insolent Texan he had been compelled to withhold his hand on account of a foolish promise to Bones – and, when they rode up on Keck again, all his steers were in the river and Penny was there to save Jim Keck.

For a year Hawks had waited, knowing that such love cannot endure, and now the day of reckoning was at hand. Penny was busy with her English lord, Keck with his sordid trysts, and both had forgotten him. But Hawks had not forgotten them, nor the look Keck had given him as he lolled, sleek and smiling, against the wagon wheel. Neither had spoken, but the thoughts of both had been on Penny, and the shame she had brought upon her lover. It was a look that, sooner or later, must call for its reckoning, and Hawks had waited a long time.

Three days after Bones's notice appeared

in the paper, Seldom Seen stepped in on Hawks, grinning broadly. Ever since that day when Hawks had stumbled upon his secret, Seldom Seen had regarded him with awe, and, now that his scheme was being put to the test, the burly ruffian had made him his confidant. Hawks, gazing curiously at his rough-hewn features, had learned to read his heart. It was the Indian in his blood that made him a killer. When, once out on the open plain where no one could overhear them, Hicks had told him of shooting men down like wolves, Hawks had remembered an Indian orator, giving point to his harangue by acting out his treacherous killings. With them cunning and treachery were counted as manly virtues, second only to courage in battle, and, as Seldom Seen had gone on to outline his savage plot, Hawks had listened as impassively as a Sioux.

'We hide our men in that big warehouse,' Seldom Seen now explained, 'right across the road from the bank. When we ketch 'em just right, each feller takes his man... I've spoke for Sundance Thorp. Every rustler in Coon Hole is r'aring to git in on this. They figger on blowing Bones's bank plumb to hell. And there's one man in particular I know you'd be interested in ... how'd you like to take Keck for yours?'

Hawks pondered a moment, and Seldom Seen watched him closely.

'Nope,' Hawks said. 'I'm not in on it.'

'Well, *come* in,' urged Seldom Seen 'Here's the chance you've been looking for... I hear he beat you to it with your gal. Come in with the rest of us and I'll guarantee he'll be there. I'm just back from Coon Hole, so I know.'

'No ... much obliged, Mister Hicks, but that isn't the way I work. I'll attend to Keck ... later.'

Seldom Seen's eyes glittered, and he glanced at Hawks admiringly. 'He'll be dead ... next Thursday night.'

'Oh, that's the date, eh?' commented Hawks. 'But he may not be there. Old Bones will bungle this ... somehow.'

'He's got nothing to do with it,' Hicks stated confidently. 'I told him to get out of town. Chances are he'd've skipped out anyhow ... never seen a man more skeered of gitting hurt.'

'He'll ball it up, some way,' predicted Hawks. 'Is Curly Bill coming up, too?'

'They're all coming up!' grinned Seldom Seen triumphantly. 'Even Rooster Raslem has bit.'

'The hell you say!' Hawks burst out, startled. 'I thought he'd left the country.'

'You know him?' inquired Hicks, a shadow of doubt on his face. 'No? Well, nobody else does, for that matter. He's hiding out in some cave.'

'He stole two of my horses,' observed Hawks after a silence. 'When he robbed that train last month.'

'Oh, that's what's biting you,' returned Hicks, his face clearing. 'I thought some-body told me he was your friend.'

Hawks smiled enigmatically, and Seldom Seen leaned over toward him.

'You can take *him*,' he suggested, 'and git the reward.'

'You'll get nothing!' replied Hawks. 'Too many people are in on the secret. But old Bones will be enough.'

'You sure hate that man,' laughed Hicks, rising ponderously to his feet. 'How much will you gimme to kill *him*?'

'Not a cent,' returned Hawks. 'You'll kill him for nothing before you get through with this deal.'

'I'll git 'im out of town ... that's sure,' grumbled Hicks.

Chapter Eighteen

The thought of twenty outlaws being shot down at Powder Springs had given Hawks scarcely a qualm. They were train robbers and cow thieves, the worst element from Coon Hole – but with Rooster Raslem added it was different. He was a train robber, too, but there was something about Raslem that set him apart from hardened criminals. He was a man who, in better times, would be honest. He had been honest when Hawks had first known him, but now, of course, he was an outlaw. Hawks had warned him to give up his robberies, but was that enough? Hawks thought the matter over as the fatal Thursday approached, but Seldom Seen decided it for him.

It was Tuesday evening, and Hawks had sat up late, reading, when there came a furtive knock at his door.

'Gimme that gun,' whispered Hicks, his eyes shifting uneasily, and Hawks took up the loose boards in his floor. Then he passed out the .30-30, and, as Hicks cleaned and oiled it, Hawks imagined Rooster Raslem among the dead.

Just at dusk on Wednesday evening he rode down past Raslem's cave, but no watchful head was thrust out. Hawks glanced about dubiously, then, hiding his horse, he crept up the natural stairs.

'Hey! Rooster!' he called, and, as no one answered, he squeezed in through the mouth of the cave. There stood Raslem, regarding him defiantly.

'Say,' he said querulously, 'don't you be coming here every day. Some detective is liable to git onto you.'

'All right, Rooster,' Hawks responded. 'This is the last time I'll come. And I'll go right now, if you say so.'

'Well ... aw, stop a minute,' grumbled Rooster. 'What you got on your chest? You're looking kinder solemncholy.'

'Rooster,' pronounced Hawks, 'you're a damned outlaw, and I never intended to come back here. You've thrown in with the Wild Bunch and turned wolf, like the rest of them, but I couldn't quite let you be killed.'

'Killed?' echoed Raslem, making a grab for his belt of pistols. 'Is they somebody on my trail?'

'Not tonight,' soothed Hawks. 'Tomorrow night. You go up there, and you're going to get killed.'

'Hoo,' scoffed Rooster, hanging his belt on its peg again. 'Jest listen to the boy talk. Killed!'

'I've warned you,' said Hawks. 'That's enough.'

'Warned me of what?' challenged Raslem. 'Is they anybody coming after me?'

'Didn't I tell you,' demanded Hawks, 'that if you kept at it long enough they'd hang your hide on the fence? Where are you going tomorrow night?'

'I ain't going anywhere,' denied Raslem, his eyes gleaming.

'You're a liar,' replied. Hawks. 'You're going to Powder Springs. Well, you do it, and you'll get killed.'

'The ... hell!' shrilled Raslem, but his scorn carried no conviction. 'Who told you?' he barked out suddenly.

'I came down here,' went on Hawks, 'just for old-time's sake, to warn you that this is a frame-up, and if you knew how near I came to letting you take your medicine, you wouldn't ask any more questions. What I've told you tonight is from one friend to another, and I don't want it to go any further. Goodbye, Rooster.'

He held out his hand, but Raslem jerked him back.

'Now, here, Clay,' he begged, 'I want you to do me a favor. Let me tell this to Sundance, will you? He's a damned good kid, and we've got it all framed to skip to South America together. Lemme tell you about him... I know he's got a hard name, but you don't know the circumstances behind it. He's another one of the boys that old Bones started wrong...'

'Sure, and that's just what they counted on, Rooster. You boys are not satisfied to rob all the trains in the country. You've got to have revenge on Bones. Maybe he did start you wrong, but does that give you any license to rob banks and shoot up the town? Every time I've come down here, you've been telling me how smart you were...'

'All right, I'll admit I was wrong. But I'll

tell you what I'll do, Clay ... you let me warn Sundance and I'll guarantee he leaves the country.'

'And will you leave the country, too? I'll shake hands on that, Rooster. Which way will it be ... South America?'

'After I do one more job,' replied Raslem. 'But this is damned white of you, Clay. I appreciate it.'

'Well ... warn Sundance. And good bye, Rooster.'

They shook hands gravely, and Clay rode half the night before he camped and waited for dawn. The trails were being watched, and neither friend nor rustler must see him coming back from Raslem's cave. When he arrived at the ranch house, Seldom Seen and the spy were gone, and Hawks waited for the news from Powder Springs. Seldom Seen had gone to town to slip into the railroad warehouse, and his rustler friend had returned to Coon Hole.

The news came from Seldom Seen, riding back Friday morning, his eyes red with rage and fatigue. 'I've been sold!' he cursed, as he put up his rifle. 'The Coon Hole gang never come. Somebody has tipped 'em off, and when I find out who it is...' He tapped the rifle significantly.

Hawks watched Seldom Seen ride off after he had had a few hours' sleep. Then Hawks oiled his own pistol and rifle. *He* was the man who had tipped them off, and, if Raslem had mentioned his name, he would have to pay dearly for his friendship with the outlaw. It was easy now to see how it had happened – Raslem had warned Sundance, and then Sundance had warned someone else until the whole secret had leaked out. But it had been a murderous plot at best, and Hawks was not sorry, even when he saw Hicks riding back. In order to cover up his work, Hicks had been transferred to a line camp, where he could keep in communication with Coon Hole, and his brief calls at the ranch were disguised as routine visits, to report and take back supplies. Hawks stood in the doorway, his rifle behind the door frame, until he saw that his secret was safe. The killer of men was laughing.

'Say,' Hicks said, 'what d'ye think spilled the beans for us? Why, Sundance Thorp had a dream.'

'A dream?' repeated Hawks. 'What kind of a dream was that?'

'A damned bad dream ... dreamed his men were all ambushed while they was robbing Bones's bank ... ambushed and all killed, except him. Heh, heh.' He dropped down in the doorway. 'If any of 'em was killed,' he went on reflectively, 'it would've been Sundance himself... I had a bullet marked for him. But talk about your luck. The whole outfit would've been beefed, if it hadn't been for that dream. The night before he was r'arin' to go, but when he come down in the morning, out of the cedars where he sleeps, he was ag'in' it and ag'in' it strong. They was going to go anyway, and, when he seen he couldn't stop 'em, he told 'em about this dream. The white-livered skunks ... every one of 'em weakened. Right there I lost fifty thousand dollars.'

'Well, you'd've drunk yourself to death,' Hawks predicted consolingly, 'so maybe it's all for the best, after all.'

'Mebbe so,' grumbled Hicks. 'Never could keep no money. But I'll clean up on that outfit, yet.'

He clumped into Hawks's room where, with a book of cigarette papers before him, he began the only writing he knew. On each square of white paper he drew a striking serpent and spelled after it: SELDOM SEEN.

'That'll fetch 'em,' he said, half to himself. 'Going to send out some notices,' he went on, speaking now to Hawks, 'but, by gosh, I can't get over that dream. And the next day one of their look-outs came galloping in from Powder Springs and told 'em the whole business had been framed. My Gawd, when I come away, Sundance Thorp was a tin god. Anything that he dreamed, they'd do.'

He chuckled to himself and went on with

his writing, wetting his pencil as he thought out brief messages.

'He dreamed,' he said at last, 'that they was all ambushed at Coon Hole. Something funny about these dreams.'

'I hope he keeps on having them,' observed Hawks. 'It'll save you a lot of work.'

'Something curious going on,' remarked Seldom Seen impressively. 'I'll find out what's behind it soon. Them women-folks down there have been raining hell lately ... mebbe Missus Payne had that dream.'

'Oh,' responded Hawks, 'yes, very likely.'

'You've heard about it, hey? She's quit the old man and throwed in with Sundance Thorp. Now it wouldn't surprise me if *she* had that dream about an ambush and general killing in Coon Hole. She wants to get Sundance away before old Payne shoots a hole in 'im, so she's liable to dream 'most anything. Another fellow down there has had some bad dreams, too ... Keck's wife took a shot at him.'

He glanced up knowingly, but as Hawks remained silent, he returned to scrawling his notices.

'Heard you had it in for Keck,' he remarked.

'Yes,' Hawks admitted, 'I have.'

'You'll be glad to hear this, then, if what else I heard was true ... I mean about him and her. She came across that scalp lock that he keeps hid in his war bag, and it had a new lock on the end of it. Black hair, understand? And Pearly Payne, that went away, was the only woman in these parts with black hair. So Missus Keck took a shotgun and run him off the ranch, and she's living there now with that Englishman.'

He went on writing without looking up, and Hawks stared straight at the wall.

'Here's a notice I wrote for Keck,' spoke up Seldom Seen cheerfully, flipping the paper across the table. '"Git or I'll skelp ye," it says.'

'Pretty good,' nodded Hawks. 'How do you send them?'

'I leave 'em on the piano,' answered Seldom Seen grimly. 'That throws the big scare into their black hearts. I sure do hate a cow thief.'

'And then what?' inquired Hawks impersonally.

'In about a week,' said Hicks, 'I'll be back for my rifle. One warning is all they git.'

'And what about Keck? Do you think he'll go?'

'I hope so. I wouldn't like to kill him.'

'You wouldn't!' rejoined Hawks, suddenly yielding to his resentment, and Seldom Seen smiled at him wisely.

'Do you want me to kill him?' he asked.

Deep down in his heart Hawks felt himself convicted by this man who was a killer for pay. That was just what he wanted – to have Keck got rid of – although he had never admitted it, even to himself. But Seldom Seen, from his experience with others, had read his secret thought. This was the one particular wish that he had learned to interpret, and, as Hawks hesitated, the killer's face changed.

'Makes no difference,' he declared. 'I use my own judgment. I kill 'em when they need to be killed. But if a man treats me white and I think he's a gentleman...'

'I see,' nodded Hawks. 'You spare him.'

'By grab, yes,' blustered Hicks, getting up.

'Well, you go back to Bones and tell him from me that I'm through with this whole business, right now. It's men like you, Hicks, that make crooks of us all. Just having you around here has made me so damned low that I half wanted you to kill Keck in my place. But I can kill my own snakes.'

Hawks opened the door, and Seldom Seen passed out, a little dazed but grinning broadly.

'I may kill him yet,' Seldom Seen said.

Chapter Nineteen

In the calm before the storm that was soon to burst about him, Clayton Hawks fell prey to black thoughts, and if in turn he cursed Bones and Penny and Keck, it was not to excuse himself. Like the shadow of a cloud, evil had seemed to hover over him and now it seemed to him that he had taken the color of his surroundings. Whichever way he looked, there was no course that was blameless, no escape from the cloud's shadow. For a year he had held back and dallied and compromised until now he was left without a friend, and, when the blow should fall and the rustlers were killed, he and Bones would be marked for revenge. How much better it would have been if, like his father before him, he had cut a clean line from the start. But first Penny had shamed him, and then Bones had had his turn, and then Keck had poisoned his life with thwarted hate. He was broken by inaction, worn out from doing nothing, and even yet he dallied and compromised.

His father would have ridden down and called Keck to an accounting the day he heard Penny was free, but it made Hawks's heart sick to contemplate the depths to which their unholy love had brought them. Except for the name they had never been husband and wife, and after the first home building they had returned to their old natures – the one as faithless, in her heart, as the other. Yet, if he rode in and killed Keck, it might still be said that he did it for love of Penny; and if not, if he let this woman stealer go unpunished, they might say he was afraid. Was it not a lesser shame, then, to hire a trained assassin and have him kill Keck for a cow thief?

While he still sought the answer, the trained assassin came back, and Hawks knew his purpose from afar. When Seldom Seen had gone, he had left his war bag behind him, and now he was coming for his rifle. All the instruments of his trade had been concealed from his associates – to them he was only a rollicking cowboy – but when he slung that .30-30 to the tree of his saddle, he would become as dangerous as a rattlesnake. With that under his knee he would ride forth a killer, to make good each illiterate threat.

'I'll take that rifle now,' he said as he drew rein before the ranch house, and Hawks saw the killing in his eyes.

'All right,' he answered, but as he went to get the war bag, Seldom Seen followed close behind him. He seemed, in this new mood, to be suspicious of some treachery, or perhaps it came from overwrought nerves, for, as he took out the carbine and cleaned and oiled it again, he began talking, half to himself.

'Well, I warned 'em,' he said. 'I told 'em to hit the trail and I told 'em I'd kill 'em if they stayed. Damn a cow thief anyway. I hate the very sight of one. That Curly Bill has took cover with the Paynes.'

'Yes?' responded Hawks politely.

'He had more guts than most of 'em ... they left there on the run ... but Curly Bill and Keck stayed. I warned 'em, the both of them, that Seldom Seen would sure git 'em. Let 'im try it was all they said. Got too many horses and cattle to go off and leave 'em ... mebbe they think this is all a bluff ... but Curly Bill is at Payne's where he can look after their Coon Hole stuff, and Keck is up on Black Mountain. Got a holdout up there ... log cabin built by rustlers just over the top of the peak ... and the first man that comes up there over either trail Keck swears he'll shoot him on sight. I helped him move up there ... he thought I was going north ... and he ain't got grub for three days. Payne's sent out for more, but the old man won't pack it up to Keck ... feeling sore over losing his wife. She pulled out over the Robbers' Trail with Sundance and the rest of 'em. Coon Hole is as empty as a graveyard.' He held his thumbnail for a mirror and looked down his polished gun barrel. 'They're afraid of me,' he muttered angrily. 'Well, this is the dirty end of it ... got to kill 'em, that's all ... and I sure hate the sight of a cow thief.'

He picked up his belt and examined each cartridge, moving the most perfect ones up to the front, and, as he worked on, half oblivious of the man who stood listening, he called down curses on all cow thieves. It seemed a kind of war song to rouse up in his heart a hate for the men he was to kill, and, when he had finished, he rose up quickly and departed without a word. Hawks watched him ride away on his tough buckskin pony with the pack horse tied to its tail, and then a new hush seemed to settle over the silent prairie as he sat in the doorway and waited.

Hawks stood it for two days, but at daylight on the third he was well on his way to town. It was the same hard-packed trail that his cowboys always took when they started for Powder Springs to get drunk, but when he reached the rim and looked out across the flat, he saw mounted men scouring the plain. In twos and threes, riding in different directions, they seemed to be hunting some trail, and, when they gathered in a knot above a spot near the railroad, Hawks knew there had been another hold-up. This was the posse out cutting for sign.

He put spurs to his horse and rode across the flats to where they came galloping south, and, as the posse approached, he made out Bones with his little hat, well up in the lead as usual.

'What's the matter?' shouted Hawks, riding forward to meet him. 'Another train held up?'

'No! They robbed the bank!' Bones yelled back angrily. 'What the hell are *you* doing out here?'

'I was going into town, if it's any of your business. You seem kind of peevish this morning.'

'Aw, you make me tired!' Bones cried, almost in tears.

'They got his thirty thousand,' explained a deputy.

'Yes, and they blowed the whole damned bank down,' cursed Bones, fighting his horse. 'I'll knock your head off, you wall-eyed old skate!'

Hawks rolled his eyes at the poker-faced under-sheriff, and they fell a few paces behind.

'Slipped one over on him that time,' observed the under-sheriff grimly. 'Remember that fake bank robbery they framed up last week? The gang was too foxy for him, but about the time Bones quit looking for 'em, they come back and grab his thirty thousand. Six men ... four men, heading for

Coon Hole.'

'You'll never catch 'em,' prophesied Hawks. 'How'd they work it?'

'Two came down from the north and four from Coon Hole ... or that's the way it looks, from their tracks ... and they camped up the railroad from Powder Springs. Then they came in, sometime last night, and robbed the bank, blowing the whole front end out when they left. Looks like they just did it out of cussedness. We dug around there for two hours, thinking they'd been scared off by the explosion and hadn't broke into the safe, but it was just the other way. They robbed the safe first and touched off the dynamite afterwards. We trailed 'em to their camp, but the tracks are all chowdered up ... here's four of 'em, heading south. Couldn't find where the other two went to.'

'Yes, but those other two may have all the money. And there's no use following anybody into Coon Hole.'

'I know it,' shrugged the under-sheriff, 'but you can't talk to Bones. He's fighting his head like a mule.'

'He's crazy,' pronounced Hawks. 'I'm not going to tag after him. Let's go back and look for more tracks.'

'Go ahead,' nodded the under-sheriff. 'He'd get sore if I quit him. But it's no use ... look how them horses were galloping.'

Hawks dropped back to the rear and then

out of sight and followed back on the out-laws' trail. They had been galloping fran-tically, over gulches and through bushes, straight across country for Irish Lake and Coon Hole. He tracked them back to their starting place, a hidden camp near the railroad where some water had gathered in a mud hole, and then along the right-of-way to town. There the tracks were trampled out, and, giving up the useless search, he joined the crowd at the bank. It had evidently been a thorough and carefully thought out job for the explosion of the dynamite had toppled the whole front wall in, thereby covering up the safe. And the alarm and confusion that had followed the explosion had covered up the robbers' escape as well.

The wrecking and robbery of the town's one bank had thrown Powder Springs into a turmoil, and the fact that the robbers were, in all probability, former patrons did not temper the wrath of even the saloonkeepers. A Vigilance Committee was being formed to clear the town of suspicious characters. All the citizens were going about armed, and, knowing that two horsemen had not fled with the rest, a search of vacant buildings was on. But all this was brought to naught when, late the following evening, the first of the returning posse reached town. The four horses they had trailed turned out to be pack animals, purposely stampeded to lead them astray, and when, near Irish Cañon, they finally came up to them, the wild creatures had stampeded again. After a chase of several miles it was discovered that they were bronchos returning to their range in Coon Hole. When they were finally roped, nothing was found in the packs but some greasy old plates and frying pans that had been attached to the packs to add to the clatter of these tins, and the only clue to the identity of the robbers was in a picture on one of the dishes. Scratched with a fork on the sooty bottom of a frying pan was the face of a man, done in letters. Clayton Hawks took one look and turned away – it was the moniker of Rooster Raslem.

This, then, was that last job that Raslem had stayed over for, even after Sundance Thorp had fled, and, after seeing that solemn visage spelling R-A-S-L-E-M, Hawks went back to his hotel room in disgust. He had risked his life, and his good name as well, to save Raslem from the consequences of his acts, but so vindictive was Raslem's hate that he had returned, apparently single-handedly, to wreak a belated vengeance on old Bones. A very complete and fitting revenge it had been, depriving Bones of nearly forty thousand dollars, and, after blowing in the whole front of the bank building, Raslem had disappeared without leaving a trace.

The next morning at daylight the posse

rode back to Raslem's camp to investigate his mysterious disappearance, and, seeing the two sets of horse tracks that led in from the north, Bones himself made the suggestion that they backtrack. With over twenty-four hours' start any pursuit would be hopeless, for the Hole-in-the-Wall country lay north, but they had not gone far when the mystery was spelled out to them as plainly as tracks can write. Some two miles from the railroad there was a trampled piece of ground and two sets of discarded horseshoes to explain it. From there, leading off north, were the tracks of two barefoot horses, while the south-bound tracks had disappeared.

Raslem had camped at the mud hole with two sets of horses – his own mount and a gentle pack animal, and four Coon Hole bronchos. Before he robbed the bank, Raslem had reversed his horses' shoes – hence the tracks that seemed to come in from the north. Then, safely away from camp and the zone of sign cutting, he had wrenched off the tacked-on shoes and headed north barefoot, bearing away Bones's forty thousand dollars. The pursuit ended right there, and, as Bones turned back to town, the posse avoided him, wild-eyed. He was cursing Rooster Raslem with such venomous rage that they looked for God's lightning to strike him dead.

Through these events Hawks lived in a trance. He took an active part in the hunting, but he kept thinking of Keck.

Chapter Twenty

When Seldom Seen turned killer, he quit the trail like a wolf, but Coon Hole sensed his presence. No one had seen him to know him, yet they knew he was there, for when the warnings had been distributed, Seldom Seen had stalked among them, dropping cigarette papers in their blankets. Every man had been suspected when he stood there in their midst, but least of all honest John Hicks, and even yet, to those who hid, Seldom Seen was a disembodied spirit. He was coming, that they knew, but what manner of man he was no one but John Hicks could say. And John Hicks was gone, warned out of the Hole by this same Seldom Seen they all feared, and to preserve his incognito he was prepared, when he took the trail, to kill every rustler that he met. That was his system – he ran amuck.

Day was dawning in Coon Hole when he came out above the Payne Ranch and lay flat on a high reef of rocks, and now, as always, he was as nerveless and capable as when he was riding bronchos. He had had his can of coffee before the day broke, and, as Mary Payne came out and got chips to cook breakfast, he was content to watch her and wait. She looked up often at the ridge as she hurried to and fro, and men's voices could be heard from the house, but Curly Bill and the Paynes kept close indoors, for it was the dangerous hour of the day. Only a woman was safe to come and go, with Seldom Seen in the hills, and of the three women Telford Payne had brought to Coon Hole, Mary Payne was the only one left. Mrs Payne had run away with Sundance Thorp, and Pearl had died covering up her shame.

There was quiet as breakfast was served and eaten, and then Charley Payne came out. He was a tough boy, but weak, and, although he consorted with the rustlers, he had escaped the general warning. So also had his father, for Seldom Seen used his own judgment, but notwithstanding Telford Payne remained inside. Charley came out whistling and walked across the flat to the round corral where some wild horses were penned. They were bronchos that he had driven up the day before to be halter broke and later ridden, but at each cast of the rope they circled the corral with a sudden thunder of hoof. Again and again the boy roped at them, and missed, and at last Curly Bill stepped out – the sound of the horses'

223

running had gotten into his blood. He stood a while looking, then stepped back inside, and came out with a rope in his hand. Seldom Seen picked up his rifle and waited.

Curly Bill walked out laughing and stood at the gate, whirling his rope with a practiced hand while Charley beckoned him on.

'Come on, Curly!' he called. 'Let's ride that big roan. You son-of-a-bitch, you're afraid to get on him!'

'Ah ain't afraid of nuthin',' answered Curly Bill recklessly and started out across the flat. The ground was open from the house to the creekbed, except for the round corral, but as Curly Bill stepped out, Charley Payne came running toward him directly in the line of fire. Seldom Seen watched them across his rifle sights, unruffled by the interruption, until they met, and Charley turned back. Then, as they walked along together, each swinging his loop and laughing, Curly Bill pitched forward and fell dead. A rifle cracked from the reef of rocks above, and in the breathless silence that followed Charley Payne started running across the flat. At each stride of his thin legs he leaped to one side, expecting a bullet in his back, and so frantic was his panic that he clung to the dragging rope until it caught on a bush and threw him. Seldom Seen watched him grimly until he reached the line of willows, then crawled back, and mounted his horse.

Over trails that the rustlers themselves had made he rode headlong through the cedars for Irish Cañon, and, when a messenger from the Payne Ranch came riding to spread the alarm, Seldom Seen was watching from the rim. His first shot missed the messenger's heart by a fraction of an inch, tearing off the whole front of his shirt, and, as the rustler dropped forward, raking his horse with his spurs, a second bullet bored the cantle of his saddle. The man reeled from the shock but kept on spurring, until a third shot from the rear knocked horse and rider over together and piled them up in the road.

Having cut off the messenger carrying the news of Curly Bill's death, Seldom Seen rode up the cañon in his stead, and at the rustlers' camp above he killed two men with his six-shooter, leaving their bodies among the calves they had stolen. There was a trail of blood behind him when, just before sundown, he came within sight of Hawks's ranch. Hawks saw him in the distance, scouting around behind the ridges to make sure it was safe to approach, and, when Hawks raised his hand, he came dragging in, his eyes gleaming like a sheep-killing dog's. He looked wicked, yet eager to please.

'My Gawd, Hawks,' he said, 'lemme put this rifle away before I kill every cow thief in the country. Knocked down five of 'em since sunup and let the big one go free ... he was sech a god-damned fool.'

'Yes, but where do I get off?' Hawks demanded sternly, 'if that rifle is found in my house? You can take your damned rifle and turn it in to Bones ... he's the man that put you up to all this.'

'Every man that I meet, I kill,' snarled Hicks, 'as long as I've got that rifle. You can use your own judgment ... leave me put it under your floor or... '

'All right ... put it away,' answered Hawks. With that killing look in his eye, Hicks was not a man to argue with – it was safer to give him his way.

They went in through the kitchen, and, when the rifle was safely hidden, Hawks insisted upon cooking a hasty meal. Seldom Seen paced in and out, now feeding his gaunted horses, now returning to clean his six-gun but when he had eaten and the coffee had stayed his nerves, he rolled a cigarette and began talking.

'I killed that Curly Bill,' he said, 'at three hundred yards he never moved a muscle ... and young Charley Payne that thought he was so tough took out across the flat like an antelope. It'll be a long time before that kid steals a cow... I reckon he's running yet. Then I rode up Irish Cañon to where those two Simms boys were camped. I killed some rustler from Coon Hole on the way. And what do you think those two skunks were doing? ... weaning calves in that pole corral.

'"Hello, boys," I says, "picking 'em kinder green, ain't ye?" And before they could bat an eye, I pulled out my six-shooter and knocked 'em over like rabbits. The magpies will be busy for some days in these parts, but the rustling industry is stopped. Met George Burt up the road as I was riding for Black Mountain, so I had to put his light out, too. Nothing but a cow thief, anyway. But the first man I should've killed ... this son-of-a-bitch Keck ... by grab, Hawks, I couldn't do it! They's something about that feller ... I don't know what it is ... that makes me kinder like him. He's a rustler, I know, but he's good-hearted.'

Seldom Seen sat back in his chair and inhaled deeply from his cigarette, watching Hawks through the cloud of smoke.

'I know you don't like him,' he went on bluffly, 'but Hawks ... here's the way it was. I warned this man Keck along with the rest of them, but, hell, he wouldn't scare. Said the man didn't live that could run him out of the country and went up to that cabin under the peak. I went along with him to kinder argue the matter, him thinking I was going north myself, but *he* wouldn't argue ... jest laughed and showed his teeth ... so I went off and left him the next day. But

227

before I left, I made me a little path right up through them quaking asps in front of his cabin, and today, when I went back, I left my horse in the quakers and slipped up to within a hundred yards of his door. Well, what do you think that son-of-a-bitch was doing? He was standing there curling up his mustache!'

Seldom Seen laughed harshly and rolled another cigarette 'You *can't* kill a man like that.'

Hawks blinked and looked straight ahead.

'Well, maybe you could,' Seldom Seen conceded, 'but I'd killed five already, and I went back and hid both my guns. Then I let out a yell and came riding up the trail, and, by grab, *he* couldn't shoot, either. He was damned glad to see me ... to tell you the truth ... being plumb out of tobacco for one thing, and, after we'd had a smoke, he came right out and told me what it was that was keeping him in the country. He didn't mind the cows or anything else, but he was waiting to fill out that scalp lock. Seems he's got the hair of every woman in the country, with the exception of jest one gal, and I'm a goddamned liar if he wasn't staying on to try and collect her skelp.'

'Yes? And what girl is that?' inquired Hawks evenly, although his heart was thumping in his breast.

'There's only one gal left,' chuckled

Seldom Seen. 'That youngest one of old Tel Payne's. And before he left the ranch, he got the old man to promise he'd send her over with his grub. He was looking for her, today, but, of course, she won't be there on account of Curly Bill getting killed, but when she does come he won't take no for an answer ... and then he's going to ship out north.'

'She'll never come now,' spoke up Hawks at last.

Seldom Seen shook his head. 'She promised to come ... not later than tomorrow ... and it seems she always keeps her word. The old man has been using her to pack grub out to these train robbers when they thought some detective was around, and Keck says she's kinder sweet on him anyway, so...'

'So you decided to let him live, eh?' sneered Hawks.

'Well, for Christ's sake!' burst out Hicks, 'ain't five of 'em enough? Do you want the whole shooting match killed? And old Bones has only got twenty-five hundred dollars anyway, so what's the use of killing any more? I'm only getting five hundred apiece.'

'Oh, I see,' observed Hawks with a malevolent smile. 'Well, I've got some bad news for you, Hicks. As a matter of fact Bones received three thousand dollars ... but it's too late now, of course.'

'That son-of-a-bitch!' cursed Hicks.

'But don't let that spoil your trip ... you did pretty well, anyway. And what's five hundred dollars ... between friends?'

'Say, what's biting *you?*' demanded Seldom Seen, suddenly detecting the note of sarcasm. 'Suppose you're sore because I didn't kill Keck.'

'Oh, no,' protested Hawks, still smiling at him mockingly. 'I wouldn't want you to go against your conscience. If you think he's a good man, don't let me influence your judgment...'

'Aw, to hell with you,' grinned Hicks, getting up 'You're jealous because he stole your gal.'

'No, I was just trying to find out your idea of a gentleman. You're so easily pleased, Mister Hicks.'

'Mebbe so,' grunted Seldom Seen. 'Say, lend me a horse, will you? I'm going to Powder Springs and get drunk.'

'Not on my horse, you're not. The big drunk can wait.' He paused. 'So you think Mister Keck is a gentleman?'

'I'll go on my own horse. Say, you think you're smart, don't you? Well kill your own snakes, Mister Hawks.'

'I'll do it,' spoke up Hawks after a silence.

Chapter Twenty-One

The time comes to every man when he must follow his own conscience, regardless of public opinion. Even Seldom Seen in his profession as a murderer claimed the right to think for himself. In bitter jest Hawks had goaded him like a rattlesnake, but he insisted that Jim Keck was a gentleman. Penny had met Keck at the gates of a house of prostitution and had come away protesting he was a gentleman. It was when Clayton Hawks heard what was keeping Keck in the country that he decided to kill him.

A vision flashed up before him of Mary Payne in her garden, and the struggle was over for him. He saw her shy blue eyes gazing out from among the columbines, and his heart went out to her in pity, yet this murderer for hire had spared the life of Keck so that he could crush her as he would a wildflower. What kind of a code was this, where men were killed for stealing cattle and spared to collect a scalp lock of a woman's hair? Hawks rose up white with fury and watched Seldom Seen out of the gate, then ran to catch up his own horses. From the hole beneath his floor he drew out the polished rifle that had killed its men that day, and with Hicks's carbine beneath his knee and his own pistol in his chaps he rode off through the night, heading south.

At daylight he took the trail that led up Black Mountain, changing horses to keep up his speed, but the sun was high before he sighted the hidden cabin where Keck lay hidden and waiting. The hold-out of the rustlers was built against a bluff just under the brow of the peak, but where the snow water from above seeped out along its base, the aspens had sprung up in a thicket. On that same side the door of the cabin had been placed, perhaps because it opened on the spring.

Hawks rode down to the cabin, a blinding rage storming in his heart. He dismounted at the cabin door and called out loudly: 'Come out, Keck!'

The door swung open, and Keck, re-splendent in a yellow silk shirt with a red handkerchief at his collar, came out. He was cleanly shaven, hair slicked till it shone, and obviously he was anticipating a female guest His even white teeth showed in a mocking smile.

'Hello, Mister Hawks. What brings you here?'

Hawks's answer came back hard, without tone. 'I'm going to kill you, Keck, right here, now. You're a thief ... a stinking, rotten one

... of women and cattle ... and don't deserve to live.'

Keck's features blanched, a flicker of terror flashing into his eyes as spasmodically he tore at the heavy six-shooter at his side. Hawks was too quick. Although both shots came so close together that they seemed blended into one, Keck jerked back convulsively as a bullet tore through his heart. Hawks watched without feeling as the man, already dead, sank to the ground. Without a second look at the lifeless rustler Hawks mounted and rode from the cabin.

No one ever knew who had committed the killing and few, if any, cared. Hawks deemed it best to say nothing of the matter, not through fear of recourse by Keck's friends but because in his own mind it required no explanation.

The news spread in waves, as fast as men could ride, when the body of Keck was discovered, and his scalp lock, dabbled in blood, was shown in saloons from Green River, to Rawlins and Cheyenne. But the man who had done the deed was never even sought, for another wave swept over the land. Year after year the rustlers had been getting bolder until they ruled the western counties of Wyoming, but at word of Keck's death every cattleman took courage and set about clearing his own range. Cattle inspectors became suddenly vigilant, looking through butchers' hide houses and rooting out stolen brands, and, while the excitement was at its height, William Bones rode through Coon Hole and swept it clean of strays.

The recreant sheriff of Bear County rode at the head of the posse, but it was Bones who really led them. While Bones was about it, he seized all of Payne's cattle to satisfy a mortgage he had bought up. The mortgage had cost him considerably more than its face value, but he got it back on the cattle, and, to make a thorough job of it, Bones scripped all of Coon Hole except the Payne homestead and Penny's ranch which were exempt. He had showed his hand at last, and some of the Snake River cattlemen began to wonder what was in the wind. Old Telford Payne, broken and penniless but still defiant, informed them of what he had known from the first. Every move that Bones had made, from stealing Payne's cattle to hiring Seldom Seen, had been done to get Coon Hole for his winter range, and Payne further warned them, one and all, that the time would come when they would share the same fate with him. But Clayton Hawks needed no such warning. While the posse was still in Coon Hole, he moved down from Hawks Mesa and reoccupied his whole lower range.

Of all the cattlemen who had suffered

losses from the rustlers, Hawks was the only one not seen in Coon Hole. He sent down two cowboys to rep for him with the strays and began his shove-down forthwith. It was rumored that he stayed away on account of Bones, with whom he had had words over Seldom Seen, but the wise ones intimated that Telford Payne might be right, and that Clayton Hawks might know it. Only the perfidy of his cowboys the winter before had kept Bones from taking possession of the Alkali, and what were a few strays, that could be picked up later, in comparison to losing his winter range? But, whatever the cause, Hawks stayed out of Coon Hole – and he had suddenly become very grim. Even Bones avoided him, sensing a smoldering hostility that a single word might fan into flame, but no one guessed his secret.

Being a Hawks he had his moral struggles in advance, but after the event none at all. He had done, as he conceived it, a great service to the range by ridding it of Jim Keck forever. Only once in two years had he seen Mary Payne face to face, but that time had been enough to fix forever in his mind an impression of her innocence and charm. Since then she had grown up – among outlaws, to be sure – but he knew she would not change, and, although he had missed her when he rode past the Payne Ranch, there were the hollyhocks and columbines to reassure him. As long as she loved her flowers, she was safe. Yet it had been Mary riding in with Keck's supplies who had found the stark body at the cabin, and since that day, although other men rode in there, Hawks had avoided Coon Hole for her sake. She might read the secret in his eyes.

The shove-down was well over, although the branding had not begun, and the cattle were getting located on their old range – each cow seeking out the spot where she had watered and grazed before, and the cowboys merely holding them on the range. All fear of rustlers was past, and Hawks rode back to his ranch to read and make up his sleep. Bitter memories came back to him as he lay on the couch and gazed at the papered wall – that paper had been put on by Penny's butterfly hands while she was scheming to meet Jim Keck and be free. And now she was free – living with Lord Abernathy, so it was said, unconcerned about the past.

The marriage of Penny to Lord Abernathy came soon after Keck's death, and she, the lord, and Mrs Pennyman entrained for the East. To Hawks, their departure left no regrets, except that possibly he had suffered more humiliation through their peculiar moral system than was good for his peace of mind. Not by any means the frustrated lover, there nevertheless was a peculiar void in his heart.

After a day of aimless riding he turned his horse into Coon Hole. An unsettled rest was over him. He wanted to find Mary Payne.

Over on a low knoll that overlooked the mesa she sat, nearly half hidden in the tall grass, looking silently out at the beautiful vast stillness. There he found her. She rose quickly, startled at his quiet approach.

'I didn't think you would ever come back here.' Her soft voice trembled. As she stood there, to Hawks she appeared the loveliest thing ever. He suddenly felt that he wanted her as he had never wanted anything in his life. He took her tiny hand in his.

'Mary, will you come back with me to my ranch and let me help you forget all the unhappiness you've been through?'

Her child-like eyes looked up into his wonderingly. Secretly she had loved this silent rancher who had made such a gallant and winning fight against the rustlers.

'I can't, Mister Hawks. Oh, I can't.'

Tears rushed into her eyes. Women's tears were not something new to Hawks, but coming at this time it confounded him. To Mary, this sounded like just another offer made her by the rustlers who had hung out at Coon Hole – to come and live with them.

'Then what are you going to do? You have no friends here. I'm not such a difficult person to get on with. We could be married tonight and go away for a while.'

Unfeigned amazement erased the sadness front her lovely face. 'Marry me? Oh ... Clayton ... you do mean that, don't you?'

It was now his turn to be amazed. 'Why, Mary, you didn't think I ever meant anything else?'

'No ... but I didn't think you cared for me. I'm a nobody. You're not doing this out of pity?' she asked tearfully.

His answer was to gather her soft young body into his arms.

The publishers hope that this book has given you enjoyable reading. Large Print Books are especially designed to be as easy to see and hold as possible. If you wish a complete list of our books please ask at your local library or write directly to:

The Golden West Large Print Books
Magna House, Long Preston,
Skipton, North Yorkshire.
BD23 4ND

This Large Print Book, for people
who cannot read normal print,
is published under the auspices of

THE ULVERSCROFT FOUNDATION